Fire Season

Miles Wilson

STEPHEN F. AUSTIN STATE UNIVERSITY PRESS
NACOGDOCHES, TEXAS

Manufactured in the United States of America

Cover Photo: Miles Wilson
Cover Design: Rob Wilson
Book Design: Troy Varvel

Stephen F. Austin State University Press
P.O. Box 13007 SFA Station
Nacogdoches, TX 75962
sfasu.edu/sfapress
sfapress@sfasu.edu

Distributed by Texas A&M University Consortium
www.tamupress.com

Library of Congress Cataloging-in-Publication Data

Wilson, Miles.
Fire Season / Miles Wilson.

ISBN: 978-1-62288-048-5

1. Firefighting—fiction. 2. California—fiction. 3. American West—fiction. 4. U.S Forest Service. 5. Magical Realism

In Memoriam

El Cariso Hotshots, Loop Fire, 1966
Mormon Lake Hotshots, Battlement Creek Fire, 1976
Prineville Hotshots, South Canyon Fire, 1994
Granite Mountain Hotshots, Yarnell Hill Fire, 2013

Wonder ye then at the fiery hunt?

–Herman Melville

For Paul Gleason

I

I think it is fitting, even, perhaps, necessary, that as I begin this, rain has begun to fall. A simple rain, unaccompanied by wind, without thunder. It will pass, east to the desert, the pungence of a new season riding the air till morning. Beneath the rain, the old discontinuities: San Andreas, Santa Sangre, Soledad, Sierra Madre, Lytle Creek—shape-shifters wound deep, continents in transit on either side. Above the fault lines, green is coming in; this week the yucca will be blooming.

It has been a long time, thirty years almost. Montana, Oregon, Colorado. Grazing rights, timber rights, water rights. I defend the land from its people, and sometimes, arrogant, defend the land even from itself. Thirty years. Time from which I have won a wife, three daughters, and the right to address the Rotary in the name of the Forest Service. I have multiplied my Civil Service rating, learning to manipulate staffs and budgets as fluently as I once swung a brush hook. And now I have come back, at the beginning of another summer, to where I began. Catlow District, Santa Sangre National Forest, full circle. It is a strange thing, such a symmetry.

I am not especially liked by other rangers. Defunct English major, I came to forestry after starting out with books. I read them still: biographies, novels, philosophy, even poetry. This is considered odd and I do not talk much about it. At small, remote ranger stations your life is a party line; word gets around.

I am, I think, a measured and watchful man. A lucky man. I have my health and work I value; the government promises me a comfortable future. I have a wife as certain and surprising as current in a mountain stream, and daughters whose precious ordinariness will make their way smooth.

Still, I understand how all this can tilt away, how near, always, the coast of darkness. Our continuities are threaded on precarious lines, strung between the pit of the past, the prowl of the future. Books are outriders that bring me this news. They confirm messages from memory, freighters adrift from my past bearing cautionary tales. Others hoard food, invest in gold, build bunkers, assemble arsenals recommended by doomsday magazines. I stock my library, in the expectation that the overturnings of our lives will be personal, not political.

I suppose this has given me a certain gravity. When I look at myself, I must count the cost in spontaneity and delight. My wife, mostly at right moments, leaves a feather on my plate at breakfast. "Lighten up," is the message. From their mother, my daughters learn to tease me into forgetfulness. In gratitude, I watch for all of us, keeping the news to myself.

My subordinates—confident and inert statisticians—calculate my difference quickly. Although I am easy to work for, the ambitious request transfers when they understand that no one will make his career by riding my horse to the top. Those who have muffled themselves in the Forest Service see me as no threat and try to get away with as much as they can. My superiors are also divided in their opinions. Good forest supervisors regard me as diffident; others find me aloof, no team player. At regional meetings, my roommates find reasons to drink with others. Then, too, we write to each other a great deal in the Forest Service. And I'm afraid the wry tone and civilian vocabulary, without which I early on found reports and memos impossible, are not often well-received. And the stories, yes, of course, the stories have followed me one way or another.

It is this accumulation that brings me, David Service, tonight—installing the cargo of a thirty-year career, poking through files full of print outs, directives, reports, trying to remember who I must see tomorrow—to the certainty that I have come to the desk from which, one day, I will be retired.

The office is not as I remembered, but I had expected that. A rotation of rangers since Oscar has converted it into what I suppose is an efficient working space. These days, the Forest Service gives seminars on such things: "Mid-Management Office Habitat: Structure and Function." The room feels like the office of some corporate accountant, as though what is transacted here has nothing to do with the land. Oscar ran the district from the field, and this office, which he worked in largely at night, looked always at random, as if he were perpetually moving in.

His filing, however, was impeccable and abundant, the result of a secretary who came to work for the Forest Service out of high school and is still here. My secretary now, Miss Proate—yes, Miss—is at once deferential and proprietary. She has inherited me, and is prepared to make everything operate properly as soon as I acknowledge her prior claims here. Neutered but uncorrupted by this long and singular employment, she has preserved the least of the district's relics with the zeal of a monk. When Gifford Pinchot calls us all to account at last, we may be judged by these archives.

The station log, passed from ranger to ranger, is the only continuity older than Miss Proate, running back to the district's beginning in 1923. I am the eleventh ranger on the Catlow, custodian of these fault-block mountains that will one day shrug me or one like me away. Oscar understood this, yet he set himself to steward what could otherwise be ruined on a human scale. Other good men have labored here; Oscar Steenbergen paid attention here—to the large and the nuanced—and his attentiveness came to be, I think, finally the same thing as love.

"24 June, 1952. The East Fork bridge washed out in the storm two nights ago—4.03 inches in the gauge at Crystal Lake. A boxcar of a boulder took out the 12x12's like they were tinker toys. Whitey and the crew can reroute the trail downstream to the old ford. The remnant stand of madrone where Broken Fork comes in lost a few trees in the blow, but the rest are putting on good growth."

"Broken Top lookout is complaining about leaks in the roof and threatens to stop losing to me at chess if I don't send someone up to fix it. Three spot lightning fires up Hardy Ridge before the rain took care of them. We got out lucky—this one pulled out the heavy artillery. If we'd caught a dry lightning bust, we'd have been in considerable trouble. Lord, for the rain in September—something to stand with us against the Santa Ana."

But I'm already out of step. The log is to be my book of days; I intend to read each entry on its anniversary. By September, I will be into the rhythm of the season, ready for whatever Oscar found in him to say about Backbone.

I should be getting oriented; I promised myself that when I came in tonight. There is the demonstration timber harvest proposal, an environmental impact statement on chemical toilets along the Crest Trail, Recreation's request to send their summer aides to law enforcement school. I know most of what will be said; only the figures change. Still, I should read it.

Instead, I indulge my homecoming, prod the past, testing the patch I have sewn over it, seeing how much will leak through. Only the log is off limits. In one of the file drawers was a folder indexed Dalton Hotshots, Media Supplement, 1967. In it, I found a packet of articles from the *Los Angeles Times*, some clippings from several local papers, and crew photographs, going back intermittently to the mid 1950's. After locating myself at last, astonished at the youth who looked spotlessly back at me, I turned to the other faces. And from the faces to the stories. And back to the files where there was nothing more. Then rising up, like splinters working their way out, the voices, and the voices assembling themselves into words:

. . . *and when it could make sex again with wind it came and that was time ago fifteen years. It burned up Cable's arm and what you call soul, it burned up my brother and other men, it burned on long hills and long canyons. But it gave a mistake about our strength and it lost courage at one important place. We could not finish the whole. The whole escaped away from us. And it has healed itself; it is strong again now, white and yellow and blue. Its doom runners come already before it. Whose name cannot be said prepares its way.*

. . . *Americans think history is George Washington being hauled across some river while the band plays Yankee Doodle. The ruling class knows that history is whatever lie you want to invent, as long as you can sell it. It's one of the slickest lies they've managed to pull off.*

. . . *I don't want to but I keep on going closer and then all of a sudden there's this thing between me and the tree without any clothes on and he turns around and I see it's him except he's just white skin all over without any way to breathe or talk or see or anything. But it's him all right. He makes me do something bad with him and then he makes me look up in the tree and instead of leaves there's lizards, millions of lizards. They've all got their eyes sewed up shut and they're shivering like the wind was blowing them but I know the real reason is they're on fire inside just like the tree. And I know I got to tell Mr. Cable and then I know I can't because the last lizard I see looks like me.*

. . . *Already he draws my breath and I must make my own way. I can not make little piles of myself for you. I am not hands empty of weapons, but I must gather the luck of all my person against what comes. I can not help you now. Now, you can not help me. Make yourself small and close to the earth—a chip of rock, a bead of air, the beetle's underside. Do not be looked for.*

. . . A diversion, out here in Gaza, but not necessarily harmless; who enters the gods of nature is beyond restraint. Someone that sincere and extravagant. . . . He's erratic enough the calculus of human probability doesn't apply. Everyone is dangerous. Yes, even you, my sentinel friend. But a man whose deviations plot out on no human curve has somehow fooled the odds, has become utterly corrupt. There is no way of predicting what he is capable of.

. . . Someone screaming "no no no no no no no." A voice so gone in terror and pain it seemed unshaped by a human mouth.

So the old patch is porous, more sieve than seal, and it leaves me, no swimmer, with the rising past, appalled. "Appalled." That strikes me as the kind of apocalyptic language I have come to expect whenever Earth First! finds me out as responsible for a stump somewhere. But there it is, and though I would like to temper it, I cannot.

I come to the past then, to memory, one memory: a root, a wound, a puzzlement. It is the vivid center to which the rest of my life has been perimeter. And it is something so distant, so foreign to me, that it happened not only in a severed past but to a different man. Suppression, I learned early, was unmanageable. I worked out what I could, learned to leave the rest alone. I do not talk about it; even my wife knows only the envelope of facts.

It has been, often, no more than a twinge, a joint that aches in certain weather. And it has felt like shrapnel, wedged against a vital organ beneath a polished scar. There were the dreams, of course, but in time their weather congealed into seasons that became part of my own internal rhythms. I had reached a point of poise, what had been a functional accommodation. If I were the last, as I have always been, to contain this past, it no longer seemed to impress any special charge on me. One might imagine Ishmael gone inland, crewing barges on the Erie Canal, playing whist with his father-in-law, grown portly on the commonplace. I was sure enough to accept this position, come back to the memory's source, past believing it could demand an account of me.

It is no figure of language that gives this past independent life; it has sustained, embedded in me, motions of its own as vivid and deceptive as the fire and the crew it repeats. That the photograph and those splinters of words should rekindle it at a touch leaves me uneasy. For I come to it now with only old habits, my caution, and whatever luck a man earns in getting through fifty years.

Still, I am pragmatic. I will saddle up any nimble metaphor; ride it until it drops. If this is an infection, then I must open it up, let the pus drain, the light and air penetrate until this history may be understood, healed.

To put it another way, setting no limits for memory is, I believe, common professional advice in such matters. The memory spreads, enlarges as it will, finally illuminating or burning out what it must. But I haven't much confidence in my own inner country's prospects of regrowth; maybe I haven't enough country left to risk. Yet somewhere at memory's blind center or ashy edge is what I must know to name it right, set this past in order, find what the line of my life is anchored to. Perhaps this is why I have come back after all. Perhaps at fifty it is time to know the truth.

Large words, a large risk. But language is a familiar comfort as I turn to this alone with what I know—alone, more, with all I need to know.

So the picture is here. The faces are distinct, no one had moved, but they conceal much. Our names, ranged in cutting order like the figures, offer a more straightforward beginning. And I need straightforwardness as a foothold.

Robert Cable, Jimmy Graystart, Mike Mundeen, Donny Cavenaugh, Randy Kruger, Carl Cominsky, George Perez, Dean Snead, Larry Calendar, David Service, Peter Jarvis, Peter Moya, Gerald Orem, Scott Stinson, Nelson Stonecrofter, Dick Pitkin.

Miss Proat had printed "superintendent" below Cable's name. And even that early, at the end of fire school, in the misting rain that comes to the Santa Sangres in early June, only Cable and Jimmy seemed dense, three-dimensional, faced into the withering heat of August.

Bob Cable, superintendent, super, sup. There was a leanness to him, an economy so stringent he might once have been a Puritan. He had hammered himself down until purpose was all that remained. In Korea, he dragged himself through two hundred yards of snow and got the machine gun that was killing his squad. It cost him some of his body along the way.

In the photograph, the fitting on his left elbow is covered. The first day of fire school his sleeve was rolled above it, but its presence, which might have been grotesque or sinister or embarrassing quickly resolved into merely a tool. The end of the fitting was a modified vise, and that first morning it held a cup of coffee. He sipped it and watched as we strung ourselves out around the mess hall. He finished the coffee and lit a Camel before he said anything.

"Let's get clear of the bullshit first. Most of you can count to two, and maybe some of you figure you got a cripple running this show. Well you're half right. You got any doubts about which half, I want to hear them." He waited, then went on.

"About this school—nobody ever learned to fight fire behind a desk, but I don't run the Forest so they'll get their school. I don't like green crews, but I've got one of those too. Mundeen here, Cominsky, Pitkin, Jimmy; they're the only ones that know shit about fire."

Somebody shuffled. Cable swivelled toward the noise.

"I can see some of you are going to be down the road kicking cans before you learn how to put out a match." The movement stopped.

"And one more thing." Cable squeezed the words out. "Dalton has never lost a line. Not one line in fourteen years. It takes men to do something like that. You measure a man against a fire, you find out what he's put together with. Sixteen hours on the line, no food, out of water, snot baked in your nose like a brick, eyes shot from the smoke, cramped up and swearing you'll never do this again as long as you live—that's when you find out who has it and how much of it he's got. You sign on with Dalton, you sign on with the Marines of the Santa Sangre. Anybody who sticks is going to make it because he learned one thing—he learned how to hate fire like you hate a man."

The first week of the first season. We started with twenty-seven, trained at the Benbow tanker station. Each night, there were fewer cars in the compound. Some men were not physical, others inept with tools, and one, massively strong, was too cumbersome to scale the ridges. Those who splintered under Cable's harrowing went too. And he pressured us all, crowding us against the time when buckling would mean losing a line:

"Cavenaugh, you don't chop with a hook. You want to hack on something, go find a Boy Scout hatchet. Slice with it. Slice!"

"Perez, get Pitkin up on your back there, boy, and see if you can't get up the hill and back before I finish my coffee."

"Jarvis, you're a college boy. How long does it take sixteen men to cut a hundred chains of line in medium bitterbrush and light chamise?"

"Orem, it's not the gun, it's the gunner. I can't make a turkey sandwich out of chicken shit."

Cable carved the week out and it seemed, in turn, a decathlon, fraternity initiation, boot camp. Whatever its models, the week made the first raw, decisive strokes that would shape us finally into Cable's own implement—the Dalton Hotshots.

We learned the tools: the pulaski, a muscular two-headed ax with a cutting blade for standing wood, a grubbing blade for roots. The brush hook, glory tool: precise, unique, lethal. Specially designed shovels—short-handled, small-bladed, steeply concave—scraped ground efficiently and could hurl a load of dirt eighty feet. And the McLeod, last in the hierarchy of tools, a rake-hoe hybrid that peeled the ground bare.

We learned other things too.

The theory of fireline construction: "I want Dalton line to look like the San Gabriel Freeway."

The many chances and fatal certainty of fire: "The first time you count on a fire to do anything besides roast your ass could be the last time you count on anything."

Tanker operation, first aid, mop-up, personnel policy, the organizational maze of campaign fires, helicopter tactics, fire camp conduct.

"Mother, you'd think they was setting us up to run the whole humping Forest."

And, always, the catechism of the Ten Standard Firefighting Orders.

"Jarvis, number seven."

"Stay alert, keep calm, think clearly, act decisively."

"Be alert. What the hell does daddy send you to college for? Give me twenty, on your fingertips."

A team from the forest supervisor's office came one afternoon. They showed slides and films and talked generally about the Forest Service, about the Santa Sangre National Forest, about how we fit in. The public information officer, a healthy-looking blonde packed robustly into her uniform, commanded our absolute attention. Her brisk delivery was underclothed with her sultry sense of that. The Forest fire control officer talked about the explosive brush of the Santa Sangres, the rate of spread and kilotonnage of a major fire. He said a lot about safety, finishing by reciting the last Standard Firefighting Order:

"Remember, fight fire aggressively, but provide for safety first."

Cable got up when he was through.

"You get in top shape, you learn your tool, you do what I tell you. That's how you stay alive."

Late in the week we were assigned tools and went out to cut practice line. The tactics of fireline construction are not complex. Starting from a secure anchor point, working next to the fire, the crew clears a strip of ground, denying the fire fuel. The hooks go in first, pioneering the line through the brush. Pulaskis follow, taking the heavier growth, widening the line, grubbing out roots and stumps. Shovels begin the scraping, and trench the line wherever burning material might roll across. On especially bad hotline, the lead shovel moves up front, throwing dirt to dampen the fire so the hooks can work. Finally the McLeods, each man scraping an equal width, finish the line down to raw earth.

The practice, no matter how hardened a crew, is gut-wrenching work. This early in the season the cutters, mostly new men and mostly in creaky shape, floundered into the brush flailing and swearing. The scrapers, having less to master, raised a blizzard of dust and crowded the pulaskis.

Cable walked the line, saying little. Twice, he called men out and took their tools. By midday half a mile of line, forty chains, angled across the ridge. Walking back down it, measuring the accomplishment against how little each alone had done, we joked with each other, kindling into a crew. That afternoon, fifteen of us were issued gear and moved to Dalton Station.

Standing in the abrupt foothills of the Santa Sangres, Dalton was the farthest east of four hotshot stations set along the explosive south slope of the Sangres—border posts against the marauding fire, what stood between its elemental simplicity and the combustible complexity of what Calendar called the American Empire that lay downslope at our backs. Dalton's five buildings, in irreversible decline from their days as a World War II internment camp for Italian prisoners, clustered tenaciously in a flat, a tribute to the thrift of the Forest Service. Successive crews had layered the buildings with whatever paint the government had in surplus that year, and the windblasted north and west walls became institutional motley by August. The furnishings were spare, military issue. The buildings and grounds were scrupulously tidy, one fathomable fetish of government agencies.

The flat was unusual in the deeply veined foothills. Triangular, it formed the blunted end of a ridge and fell away to ravines that joined at its apex. The ridges east and west, smothering in manzanita and chamise, rose hundreds of feet above the flat while our ridge gathered up, over half a mile, into the perpendicular high country of the Santa Sangres. We shared the flat with blue lizards, ravens, jackrabbits, an occasional horned toad, and the diamondback rattlers that had survived the seasons of Cable being there.

After the week at fire school, we had another week at Dalton before our first days off. We settled in, worked the obstacle course hard, and felt out our first uneven connections as a crew.

Beginning, new to each other and the work, we measured a man by his tool and his seeding in the cutting order, from the heavyweight hooks on back. I have always been bad about names, so I drilled myself until I could recite the cutting order and a little about the men who made it up.

As Cable had complained, we had few veterans, and they were concentrated up front. Graystart, a remote and luminous Indian, had been with Dalton a long time. He cut second hook behind Cable. Mundeen was third hook. He spent his college summers here, plowing through the brush like the defensive end he played at San Jose State. Team captain, keeper of traditions, he kept the rookies humble by dispensing what he called Mundeen's thousand and one pain inflicters whenever one of us needed to be reminded of our status. Cavenaugh was the only new hook. A self-contained drifter who had logged in Oregon, he knew how to make his bunk military style and was a deadly poker player.

Kruger, Cominsky, Perez, Snead, and Calendar carried pulaskis. All but Cominsky—a capable plodder hibernating in the Forest Service—were rookies. Kruger was a teammate of Mundeen's at San Jose. He traded on this to set himself up as an old hand and was quickly disliked. Perez, streetwise from the east Los Angeles barrio, had missed going to jail so far. Snead, from the tract slums of the San Fernando Valley, had not. He had a year to go on parole. Calendar was the only one of us who took notes at fire school. He smoked perpetually, wore wire-rim glasses like mine, and hated Cable.

The scrapers, outnumbered and outmuscled by the cutters, learned to expect bantering harassment. Mundeen called us farmers, and the name stuck. I was lead shovel. Behind me was Jarvis, a sophomore forestry major at Humboldt State. Cable called him ranger, blaming him for positions he might one day hold in the Forest Service—positions Cable didn't want but could never have. Pitkin, a three-year man, was tail-end shovel. His intelligence was marginal and erratic, but he was compulsive about cleaning the last shred of brush from the line and proud to be counted on by Cable to do it.

Bracketed by the shovels, Moya, Orem, Stinson, and Stonecrofter worked McLeods. Moya, quick with his mouth and with girls, was a witty counterpoint to the surliness of Perez. Perez called him Mouse; Moya nibbled away and called him Sunshine. They had grown up together. Orem was a mild and serious student at some local junior college whose ambition was to someday manage a Safeway store. Later, it turned out that he was using the summer as a tune-up for his Mormon mission assignment. He didn't make much headway among the heathens, but we didn't do his soul any favors either. Stinson, the youngest of us by a year or so, was just out of high school and painfully novice. He brought pajamas to fire school. A puffy whiner and special sufferer of Kruger, Stonecrofter hung on through some enormous need to make it. His father owned Stonecrofter Cadillac in Beverly Hills. He didn't seem surprised when we turned Nelson to Nelly. There was a cook too, Bailey, a scurrying little man who kept a bottle in his room and seldom left the mess hall.

This is what we began with. Though it seemed unremarkable, even necessary at the time, I am astonished now by how young we were, how much we had to learn. More of us were under twenty-one than over, and besides Cable, only Graystart, Cominsky, and maybe Cavenaugh were more than thirty.

The afternoon before our first days off, Mundeen slipped into Cable's office while we cleaned the mess hall. Cable had the only phone in camp, off limits except for government business. When Mike came out, he started collecting money for a keg. His girl from last summer was still around, she was having a party that night. At twenty, parties promise much and most of us chipped in. Off standby at seven o'clock, we crowded the showers, borrowed English Leather from Moya, and roadraced the twenty miles into town.

The house was in one of those fabricated neighborhoods of Southern California. Mundeen's girl, Karen, rented it with a friend. Nine of us finally got there. Pitkin had forgotten the directions and spent the night driving Glendora, looking for our cars, passing out beer to the rookies who had ridden with him.

By the time we sauntered in with two kegs, the party was well-established. Ten or so locals were there, several in lettermen's jackets. Karen, who engulfed Mundeen at the door, looked unsettled when she saw the collection Mike had brought with him.

While some of us set up the kegs in the kitchen, Mundeen leaned against the wall by the doorway, just inside the living room, drinking a beer he had taken from the refrigerator. Kruger and Snead, also with cans of beer, stood near him. Some of the locals had finished their beers, but no one made a move for the kitchen. The level of talk had dropped and there were more edgy glances. Mike swallowed the last of his beer and belched. On a full load, he could riff the opening line of "I Can't Get No Satisfaction." He bent the can in half with his thumb and two fingers.

"Glad you boys could make it," he said cordially, tilting his head and neck as one massive piece and continuing to flatten the can. "Course with a crowd like this, you can see that the management's got to require a little cover charge. Say, five bucks a head. And when you lay your money on Randy here, have your i.d.'s handy. We sure wouldn't want to get in trouble for serving minors." He belched again, a little coda.

The challenge and sizing up had been finished before Mundeen said anything. Two of the lettermen moved toward the front door, taking their time to gesture that they could have stayed if they'd wanted. Others began to follow.

"Do you mind if we take our beer with us?" A boy in a button-down shirt looked at Mundeen hopefully.

"Guess," said Kruger.

Outside, they scuffed to their cars while we followed and watched from the sidewalk. Moya waved and shouted after them.

"Sorry you couldn't stay; drive careful."

They squealed off, one of them giving us the finger as he pulled away. We went back in, studiously casual about the rout, and began fielding the five girls who remained.

It turned into one of those parties where claims are staked quickly and slow starters end up clustered around the keg in the kitchen, wandering out now and then to see if any loose ends or more women have turned up. By midnight, half through the second keg, Jarvis, Snead, and I were getting soggy. The resident dog, a black lab puppy, had shredded a carton of paper cups on the floor. When Kelly came in, we had just burned a pan of popcorn and Snead was lobbing some darts he'd found at a punctured poster of Mick Jagger. Kelly had a bottle of Red Mountain wine, mostly gone, and a look that predicted ruins.

"Shit," she said.

"Tough tits," said Snead half-heartedly, whistling another dart into Jagger's groin.

"Don't let me slow anything down; I only live here."

Kelly fended off the puppy and shook her hair back. She was trim, almost boyish, with a lightly freckled, alert face and thick auburn hair.

Snead applauded twice, sloshing some beer on his shirt, then picked up another dart and thudded it into Jagger's cleavage. Jarvis apologized and I tried to make a joke about something. With a withering review of the kitchen, Kelly went out the back door.

Jarvis pulled some change from his pocket and we flipped. Borrowing some cigarettes from Snead, I followed her. The grass was unmowed and Kelly sat in it, back to the house.

"Hey, I'm sorry about the kitchen."

Bold with beer and knowing the return I'd get inside, so soon, empty-handed, I tried again.

"Listen, hey, I am sorry about the mess, but mostly I just wanted to sit down and finish my beer and talk. Ok?"

"Go away or I'll do your tarot."

"My what?" It was an opening, but I was too slow to fill it.

"Tarot, like in cards. They predict things. Like you're going to go away and tell the rest of the beef I'm not interested." She still hadn't looked at me.

"What if I trump your Hanged Man?" I had no real idea what this meant, but I remembered the terminology from an English course.

"You know the tarot?" She looked up now.

"No, Eliot."

"Who's he?"

"A poet."

"Oh, that one." She drank some more wine from the bottle.

"Sure, shit, I don't care, stick around if you want."

So we began, Kelly finishing her wine while I roamed around for something bright to say and finally for anything at all. Women were not my long suit. I hadn't been dealt that many hands, but each one seemed a cipher that defied design. It was Kelly, though, who leaned forward finally to laugh, feisty and chiming.

"I just had the strangest hit. Here you are, out in the middle of this pasture trying to hustle me, probably sitting in a pile of Earth's crap or about to, wondering if I'm wearing a bra, hoping the wine's loosened me up enough—the whole shuck and all I can think about is artichokes and eggs."

"Artichokes?"

"I'm hungry; it comes from drinking Red Mountain without a filter."

"Oh."

"Buy me supper?"

"Sure. Who's Earth?"

"Earth is my forty-six pound familiar who's supposed to be protecting me from all this but is probably begging popcorn or pissing on the rug. Was I right about the bra?"

"Yes."

"Well I do, sometimes. Once a year on the anniversary of my first period. To remind me that Playtex is out there just waiting for my body."

When we went back in, the party had lost momentum. Moya and a compact blonde were the only ones still dancing. Someone had found a Johnny Cash album and "Ring of Fire" was playing. Snead and Jarvis were doing doorjam pull-ups for the benefit of the girl Stinson had abandoned to throw up in the hallway. Calendar, an intense and earnest drunk, was talking to Perez on the porch. He thrust his head forward as he talked, the street light glinting off his wire rims. Kruger, Mundeen, and their girls had vanished and the beer was gone.

By three o' clock it was over. Karen and Mundeen had returned and disappeared into her bedroom. Stinson was passed out on the couch. Kelly fixed scrambled eggs which we ate among the wreckage of the kitchen.

"So tell me everything I'll need to know about you; try not to lie any more than you have to."

"Well," I finished chewing a mouthful of eggs which were a little rubbery but tasted all right. "I go to school at Pomona; I'll be a senior next year if I go back. I'm majoring in English. I grew up in Oregon and I expect I'll end up there one way or another."

"Pretty puny résumé. How do you expect to get this job if that's all you have to say for yourself?"

"What am I applying for?"

"Let's just say I'm expecting an opening. Isn't Pomona supposed to have a marching band with the biggest drum in the world?"

"That's the junior college."

"What's your sign?"

"Sign?"

"Your sun sign, you know, the zodiac. Really, where have you been?"

"Sagittarius."

"Oh well. And your favorite color?"

"Your hair."

Kelly breathed out a little laugh.

"Not bad, not bad at all for an English major. But I still think we're going to have to broaden your curriculum. Loosen you up so you talk like that all the time."

"I've always wondered what summer school would be like."

"I think we'll start with some yoga, then take you off red meat and sodium to bring your energy field into balance. We'll take it slow; I won't turn you loose on Red Mountain until I'm sure you can handle it."

And so it went—testing, playing, accumulating the pieces we needed to fit each other into place. On his way out, Moya popped into the kitchen with the blonde.

"You heard about the two Mexicans in Ripley's Believe It or Not? One had insurance on his car, and the other was an only child."

The blonde let out a fluttery giggle. Moya whispered something to her, and she gave him a drowsy, disheveled smile and a long kiss. He circled his thumb and finger at me behind her back.

I left a little after Moya. At the door, encumbered by Stinson who now had the dry heaves, I told Kelly I didn't see how I could maneuver her into a kiss. Scott's stomach was pumping like a piston.

"That's all right." She tilted her head and shook some hair free. "I'll have to do the cards, but I think we're going to be sleeping together. You can kiss me then if you want to."

Stinson lurched against me and we almost fell. At the car, as I stacked Scott in the back seat, Kelly called out from the doorway.

"Remember to call home. Mothers like that sort of thing, and I have to know exactly when you were born." And shut the door good night.

I drove back to Dalton, radio up and all the windows down. I thought about all the rigid coeds who satisfied the well-groomed admission standards at Pomona. Not giving up even a feel until they were assured that your future was manicured by daddy's business or some productive major like pre-med. Some of them looking like their bodies had given up on them in disgust; others impenetrably aloof or snatched up by superstars. This was going to be different. Kelly was going to be more like it.

"Light My Fire" came on and I cranked the volume up, singing to a summer that opened up ahead. Saturday we had our first roll.

II

The fire, the Bessie Creek, came over the radio just before lunch. Snead, Mundeen, and I had been stenciling trail signs when the radio rasped, cleared, and broadcast three shrill peals. Mundeen whooped and hurled his brush across the tool room.

"Fire traffic, fire traffic. We have a smoke in Township 15, Range 6, Section 33; the Southeast of the Southwest. Tanker one-nine, tanker one-seven, patrol one-seven, crew three respond code three. Repeat. Township 15, Range 6—."

Mundeen was already lumbering across the yard and we sprinted after him. The truck was a new Peterbuilt cabover and our gear was bunched in cutting order along the parallel bench seats in its open bed. Pistol belts, hard hats, fire shirts— we wrestled them on as the rest of the crew crammed in and we counted off for Cable. Cominsky wheeled the rig out of the yard, Cable with him in the cab. As we hit the highway, our red and amber flashers came on and the siren wound. The first surge of adrenalin peaked and left us quickened. A sense of counting for something, counting a lot, flushed us as cars pulled over and drivers waved or gave us thumbs up. Southern California, fearing much from nature, fears fire most. Mundeen called off the pistol belt check—file, canteens, headlamp, sweatshirt, Trojans—and we quickened again with the laughter of pressure.

The fire had started in a campground, then moved rapidly up a ridge.

When we got there the Rincon tanker and patrolman were working the lower flanks with water. Cable was out fast, yelling "tool up" and locking the handle of a modified hook into his vise. The cutters stood, cleared the truck, then filed past taking tools from the side compartments while the scrapers came down the ramp. In less than a minute the crew was ranged in cutting order, moving up along the tanker's hose lay. At its end, Cable circled us up. We extended our tools into the ring in allegiance to the work ahead and shouted "Dalton" against the fire. Cable's hook flashed into the brush and we began.

It was steep work, but the light growth offered little fuel. The head of the fire had topped the ridge, its tendrils working down the back slope, leaving a smoldering spread that we easily lined. Cable moved along the smoking burn at the crest, arms cocked out from his sides like a gunfighter, sizing up, watching the fire ease down the canyon. If it reached the bottom ahead of us, we'd lose it in a run up the next ridge. The canyon was too narrow and serpentine for air drops; there would be little daylight flying time left when the fire reached the next ridge where air tankers could hit it. It was going to be our show.

Cable signalled Jimmy and word passed down: bump up, hit a lick and move, scratch line. We accelerated, narrowing our line to a foot. As each man reached the top he fell out, sharpened his tool, then took some water when he had cooled enough that the need for it was not as urgent. Stonecrofter tried to sneak a quick drink and was withered by Cable. A fire crew is fueled by three things: stamina, guts, and water. On the line, water is as precious as breath and with its weight you could never carry all you needed. Cable enforced a strict economy until we learned for ourselves.

Nobody talks much on the line, even during breaks. There is little to say, and after the first hours each man is alone with exhaustion and accumulating pain. We watched back down the ridge where the tanker crew worked their hoses, dodging the rocks that came erratically down as roots burned through and let go. Then Cable warned us to space ourselves out and led us down, angling along the fire, pinching our line toward its head.

Although the slope was not as steep as what we had come up, it is difficult to work downhill. The main stems of brush are shielded from the cutters by upper branches, and the scrapers must lean and reach for ground that slants away from them. To face the hill and work backing down makes footing chancy and can bring you into range of the next man's tool. But the brush stayed light and we moved quickly, driving a four foot line toward the canyon bottom.

A few hundred feet from where we would turn and move across the head, Cable increased the pace. The manzanita had bunched into thickets, and the evening, upcanyon wind rose to encourage the fire, shifting its smoke and heat across our line. The pulse of it quickened my weariness. The fire was a magnificent impersonator: now hunting like a luminous cat, fiery whiskers setting off what they touched; now wings of flame, flaring through the brush like a candescent bird of prey. The movies at fire school caught only the crude dimensions of fire. Out here, it was constructed of baroque nuance.

When the fire started to cluster flare, Cable called me up front. I gouged dirt from the rocky hillside, hurling what I could get against the base of flames or shrouding exploding brush clumps in a dampening pall, buying the hooks a buffer against the heat. When the flames curled away from them, I scattered dirt across low flames sheeting through the cheat grass. Then we had hooked the head. Cable dropped the pulaskis back to widen the vulnerable, upcanyon flank; the fire would not move downcanyon, against the wind. We watched the last spurts of flame in the thinning light.

Working into the night, we finished the line back up the ridge. At the top, we ate the sacked food someone had brought in, then spread out to patrol the line and mop up. We gridded the burn in a line, each man responsible for a parallel strip, knocking down the obvious smokes and feeling around with our hands for the sleepers. We chopped and dug the fire out, breaking it up, mixing the embers with dirt, spreading them to cool in the night air. Dull and dirty work. I've never seen a crew do it willingly, even knowing that one seed of fire, a little wind, and the flames could blossom again beyond your line. Cable kept us at it, pulling us back to the ridge only at dawn.

Too tired to sleep, we sat smoking, finishing our water, waiting for the relief crew. Cavenaugh had a gash down his cheek where a manzanita branch had sprung back from his hook. After fourteen hours in sweaty socks and new boots, most of us were blistered. Only Jimmy and Cable seemed unmarked. Winding down, people talked a little.

"Isn't it past your bedtime, Stinson?"

"Mother, did you see Cable work out with that hook?"

". . . so she spreads them a little wider and hollers down 'Did you find your ring?' And he says 'No, but I ran into some guy looking for his

Harley-Davidson.'"

"I got some gum if anybody's got a smoke."

"Match?"

"Not since Superman."

"Your face and my ass."

"Shit."

"Jimmy, hey, how'd we do?"

"Live from the Bessie Creek burn, Johnny Cash in concert: 'Because you're mine, I walk the line.'"

"It was a simple fire. It was not important."

When Chilao relieved us around seven, we landed insults out of Cable's range as he talked to their superintendent. While state and county crews and even our own tankers were fair game, Cable had warned us against harassing other hotshot crews. Even third string pros, he said, deserved respect. We'd do our talking on the line. Chilao didn't have much to say. We'd handled the fire; they'd spend the day grubbing around in the ash looking for any smokes we'd missed.

Filing through the campground to the truck, looking tough and casual as we came past the Winnebagos, we surged again with the pride of making a real difference. We had taken the mindless possibilities of a fire and reduced them to the simple geometry of a line.

At the tail-end session the next morning, Cable was lacerating. The hooks weren't throwing their brush far enough, the pulaskis had left canopy overhanging the line, and some scrapers had pulled scorched branches across it. The trenches were too shallow, mop up was half-hearted, and a lot of people had generally dragged ass.

"Things," Cable said, "are going to get one hell of a lot hotter. You're not playing grabass at some summer camp. You either do the job right or we'll all be on our butt in the burn sucking ashes. We sure would hate to see a smart ranger like Jarvis have to do that, wouldn't we Stonecrofter?"

Whatever response Cable wanted—contrition, belligerence, resolve—must have failed on our faces. He tightened another notch.

"Candies! I've got a bunch of candy asses for a crew. Candies, cherries, culls! How the hell am I supposed to cut line around a cigarette butt? Mundeen, how am I supposed to do that? Snead... Kruger...Perez?" We finished the morning cutting practice line.

After that the workouts, which we had struggled with and then settled into, became more intense. The obstacle course was Cable's special toughener, refined over many seasons. Mundeen claimed the bones of old crewman gave the chalky tint to the powdery dirt we churned through along the course. Cable had erected some scaffolding and a platform from which he could see most of the course. It started behind the barracks, looped across the flat and up the ridge, then dropped to the west ravine, following it back to camp. The final fifty yards took us up a nearly vertical crumbly dirt bank back to the flat.

Spaced along the course were a rope climb and swing, a log carry, and a device Mundeen called Cable's cock. It was a half-inch pipe, bent in irregular angles across a small gully. The first man across each day pulled a collar after him that greased the pipe for the rest of us. Beneath was an eight foot drop to a jumble of tire carcasses and clumsy, time-taking extrication. The course ran a little under three miles and we had to finish it in less than half an hour. Stonecrofter, Cominsky, Mundeen, and Jimmy needed the full thirty minutes. Moya, a cross-country runner in high school, set the early season record at twenty-three minutes. Since we ran it after Bailey's greasy breakfasts, the course was colored with bright plastic streamers that marked where someone had thrown up. "Feeding the ants," Moya called it, inspired by Orem who seldom missed a morning until he stopped eating breakfast.

Every afternoon at two the fire weather forecast and required manning came over the radio. We listened acutely, having bet on the manning code which might either cancel standby or kill our weekend. The codes ranged from one to ten. In late June they settled around five, dropping occasionally to three which released us from standby after supper. One Friday I had drawn three in the pool and the code matched. I collected my winnings during the afternoon break, enough for a case of beer, and although we worked other people's weekends, I reasoned that one luck might lead to another. If Friday night with Kelly turned out as I hoped, Saturday morning would have to take care of itself.

I worked eagerly into the shank of the afternoon. Jimmy and I had been in the tool shed most of the day, repairing headlamps, cleaning the backfiring torches, changing water in the gallon canteens. Jimmy was something apart from the rest of us, like one of those muscular pines aging against the wind and snow at timberline, distanced from the itch and nip of yearlings. He was superb at hook. Not as explosive as Cable or overpowering like Mundeen, he handled the hook like a surgeon, wasting no motion, calm and complete as he severed malignant brush. Cominsky said he had come out in the early Fifties with the New Mexico Indian crews the government brought west for a few summers. These

Indians, establishing the Dalton legend in the Santa Sangres against long racial odds, had never lost a line. And they had rarely lost a fight. In the end, the Forest Service could no longer justify the weekly rodeo: reclaiming the crew from city and county jails; waiting out three day poker games in Riverside, three day drunks in El Monte. One season a bus took them away in October and they never came back. Jimmy was all that remained of that history and his presence pointed back to legends, beginnings from which, as a crew, we once had come.

Young men, starting out, are grateful for legends, even those they cannot quite believe. Relaying the past, they promise actions a possible future. The ordinary present is dignified by the continuity, and the chance for greatness stalks the trivia of routine. America has few opportunities for legend. We move around too much, lose touch. And our democratic mistrust of excellence has massaged our failed dreams with the balm of cynical debunking.

Jimmy himself seemed as much legend as present. Kruger called him Tonto behind his back but the rest of us, impressed by his skill and watchful distance, circled him warily and, in our own way, reverently. I had seen him sometimes with Cable, in the slack time after supper, far out on the obstacle course, miniatures moving on the bulky ridge, like figures seen down the wrong end of a telescope. Pitkin, too, seemed able to talk to him. I had tried a few times, courteous, curious, but found only opaque reticence. But it was Jimmy, late in the afternoon, who opened of his own choosing.

"Listen, on the fire, never mind Cable, you did well. Cable has to be this way." He closed his fingers into a fist.

I was surprised, pleased he had noticed me on the line.

"Thanks. I was getting pretty washed out there at the end." I grabbed randomly. "How did you learn to handle a hook like that?"

Jimmy capped another canteen and began cinching its strap.

"I learned from my brother. And I have become more by myself."

"Your brother, he was on the crew?"

"Once."

We began stacking the canteens, the room muffled in dust, heat, and the smell of diesel. Cominsky had said nothing about Jimmy's brother. And Jimmy would not, at least not now. I didn't want to let the beginning go. Jimmy had come from a world I could only faintly imagine, and at that largely in cliché. My life had been spent around those who differed from me only in degree, not kind. I was beginning to realize that Oregon and Pomona were pasteurized, homogeneous as a pane of glass. Jimmy was a real chance to cross a watershed into new country. I veered back to Jimmy himself, trying to establish some ground we shared.

"On the fire, someone asked you about it and you said it didn't matter."

"I said it was not important."

"What's the difference?"

He looked at me keenly, and though he was standing he seemed oddly for a moment to crouch, poised down the room in the husky light.

"There will be more fire and time to talk about such things. Perhaps you will find out for yourself."

I was learning already that Jimmy's responses were more riddle than answer, slanting off from the purpose of your question, often leaving you with a harder question. He did explain one thing as the afternoon ran down. I had admired his belt buckle, the whole belt really. The leather was tooled in the stylized shape of a man. The buckle, silver and turquoise worked in the figure of an eagle, formed the man's stomach. Jimmy said it was a singer's belt, but it didn't mean anything now because the singers had lost the god-chants and the people no longer listened.

We finished the last of the canteens and went in to supper.

———

III

When I left for town after supper, Mundeen said to tell Karen he'd be in after finishing with the weights. He lifted every night behind the barracks, trying to bulk up for his senior year and a career beyond that in pro ball. Scouts from Los Angeles and Detroit had already talked to him.

Pitkin caught a ride in with me, his car unwilling to start since he'd tuned it up. Besides his ambition of being picked up by the Forest Service on a permanent appointment, Dick had one other passion—miniature golf. He spent his days off at the Golden Green and last week had broken thirty-six, beating a Mr. G. I. Jacobs. The tension of the last holes pressed on him as he told me about the match, as though a forgotten detail would change things and he would not have won after all.

"So Mr. Jacobs putts on seventeen and I go 'Oh boy, that's it,' but he misses so I'm still alive. So then I have to putt—no, Mr. Jacobs holes out—and then Mr. Jacobs tries to surprise me and says he'll gimme my putt but I say no thanks and putt it out by myself. So on eighteen I figure the break perfect—you got to keep figuring cause they change the pins around on you all the time—but I just look it over and putt for the money like we say down there. Then Mr. Jacobs hits his ball like he doesn't even care and it was a five-dollar game too. I still owe him a lot of money though. Anyhow, you come on over with your girlfriend sometime and I'll take you around. It's a great game and the folks there are swell even if you don't play for money."

I said we might and wished him luck in his next match with Mr. G. I. Jacobs.

Kelly was in the front yard when I drove up, hurling a shredded frisbee which Earth mauled and occasionally returned. She was wearing cutoffs and a Celestial Seasonings T-shirt. Her legs were lean with a nice arc of muscle at the calf and knobby ankles like an affectionate remnant of adolescence.

There was the hesitant moment when what had happened at the party could have been a mistake that either of us might now renounce. Then Kelly said she hoped the intentions of a fireman with a half case of beer under his arm were exactly what they looked like. We laughed at each other and went inside. I got most of the beer into the refrigerator. Kelly was drinking wine again.

"I did the tarot on you."

"Oh?"

"I wasn't sure you'd come back, but the cards were so I just polished my navel."

"I didn't know you could do that with the tarot."

"You can't. I use wheat germ oil and a felt cloth. The navel is the true sex center of the body, never mind what they taught you in health class. You called home, didn't you?"

"Oh, sure. Five forty-three, a.m."

"Great."

"Do you read bumps on people's heads too?"

"Nope, just make them happen."

I ducked the frisbee she threw, but couldn't avoid Earth who careened off the back of the couch in pursuit.

We talked, smoked, drank, watched television.

"What's Dalton like?"

"I don't know, like a job I guess."

"Isn't it dangerous?"

"Not if you know what you're doing. Do you work?"

"Sure."

Kelly reached up and pretended to wind one ear, then leaned over and kissed me, making little ticking noises with her tongue. When I started to kiss back seriously, she made a sound like a bell and pulled back.

"I'm sorry, sir, your three minutes are up. Please deposit another quarter."

I nuzzled into her hair and ran my tongue into her ear. Kelly hummed.

"Your party is on the line."

We kissed again, and when I started touching her, Kelly leaned me back down on the couch. She ran her nail lightly up the inside of my thigh, then gave me a squeezing tickle and sat up.

"Not yet. Let's see, where were we? Oh—I don't actually work right now. When I was little, my mom got in a wreck—some guy clobbered her. I got a pinched nerve out of the deal and $20,000 that I got when I turned twenty. I'm sort of sitting on the money right now till I figure out what I want to do."

"Why not yet?"

I reached over and grazed a finger over the airy, pollen-colored hair on her thigh. Kelly took my hand.

"The first time it's very important that we're in complete harmony with our celestial alignment. Once that's set, it's good forever."

"So we wait for Christmas? Or April Fools' Day? Thanksgiving?"

Kelly squeezed my hand.

"This is too important to make jokes about. You'll see. You'll see tonight."

Late, maybe two o' clock, Kelly rocked off the couch and flicked off a Jimmy Stewart movie.

"It should have cooled down by now."

"What?"

"My room. It's almost time."

Kelly's bedroom was sluggish with heat and the smell of patchouli. I walked across to the open window and pushed it up as far as it would go. When I turned around, Kelly was in front of me and naked. The streetlight fell across the dappling of freckles on her breasts, and something came loose in me like a rigid muscle letting go. Kelly unbuttoned me while I circled a finger over the whorls of freckles and brought up the darker nipple they spiraled away from.

At her bed, Kelly reached out to a wind-up clock with luminous signs of the zodiac instead of numbers.

"Oh no." She rapped the clock on the dresser. "The damn thing's stopped. Oh shit. Oh well."

And a little later, "Oh oh oh oh oh."

After, both sweaty and smoking, the tang of us still in the air:

"I'll try to be a little more durable next time."

"Practice makes perfect. Anyway, you weren't all that bad."

"Neither were you."

"I know." She took my hand and cupped it over her breast. Looking down her body, I could see the pale crescent of a scar up her side above her pelvis.

"David, the tarot, I hope your natal chart works with it. I hope it's right, I really do."

"Does that still matter, Kell?"

"Yes. I don't screw every fireman who wanders in off the street. Really."

"OK, Kell, OK."

"I'll tell you about my system sometime. It's mostly the tarot, but I use horoscopes too and I'm starting to work in the I Ching. I'm learning to flow with it. It's hard to explain, but once you give yourself up to the current it floats you into the future. The current goes around forever—it's been past every future. I think I'm getting into synch with it; I think I'm really onto something. And I sense you're going to be an important part of it somehow."

"The more the merrier."

On the brink of sleep, I remembered to set my alarm.

Driving back in the morning, bleary with hangover, I wondered what had happened to Mundeen, glad he hadn't rumbled in as Kelly and I loosened each other up on the couch. I got to camp just after Perez, Moya, Calendar, and Snead pulled in. Cable was alone in the mess hall. There had been a small fire after we'd left, but mop up had taken most of the night. The rest of the crew was sleeping in till noon. Only Moya had more than coffee for breakfast as we measured our hangovers against the obstacle course.

We stuck together on the first part of the course, greasy with sweat, swearing at it to keep ourselves going. Calendar's face was gray, and my scum of cottonmouth turned the air I sucked in rancid. One pitch of the course dropped out of sight of Cable's tower. Snead pulled up, and the rest of us stopped with him.

"All the son of a bitch needs," Snead devoured the air raggedly "is a rifle. I bet he works the towers at Chino on his days off." Snead grabbed his forearm and jabbed a finger into the sky. "Choke on it, you one-hand screw."

None of us finished the course under thirty minutes; Perez and I barely finished at all. And the lesson was not over. The rest of the morning we spent in the sun, sharpening tools used for project work. At lunch, Cable told us our nights were our own, but we'd better not forget who our days belonged to. When Mundeen found out that I'd spent the night with Kelly, he pronounced me coxman first class and promised formal ceremonies that evening.

I worked that afternoon with Jimmy, doing what I had done wrong all morning. Cable was not satisfied with the bevel I had put on the shovels. He trusted only Jimmy to refine even project hooks to the precision they required in order to cut efficiently. My hangover was like rippling plastic, screening the day and detaching me from it, penetrated by the raw scrape of metal on metal. Near break time, a sound broke above the rasp of our files and we listened as a truck ground up the last stretch of road to the camp. Few outsiders found their way to Dalton. Even within the Forest Service, it was regarded as Cable's principality. Cable had a way of making desk rangers feel parenthetical to the real work; they found other stations to inspect.

The government pickup, shrouded in dust, bounced into the compound and stopped near the tool shed. The passenger, in immaculate work clothes, got out first. As he came around the truck into full view, I was struck by his face. One side, the left, its flesh drawn tight, had a sort of waxy luminescence, pale as frosted glass. Even with that, the man had one of those neutral faces that take shape in the mid-twenties and remain fixed for another ten or fifteen years. Without the flawed side, he would have been either bland or pretty.

He stood by the truck while Oscar got some papers from the visor. Oscar said hello and asked about Cable. Jimmy said he was in the office, but he wasn't looking at Oscar as he spoke. Holding a hook, he watched the other man whose presence, even under the weight of Jimmy's gaze, was that of one who had answered for himself any question the world could put to him. Oscar said he'd be joining the crew. His name was Martin Speyer, and he'd worked for the Forest Service on the Mendocino. While I was shaking hands, Jimmy broke off the stare, put down his hook, and said he would get Cable. Speyer watched him go, squinting into the light. Oscar said it was all right, that Jimmy didn't take to people right away. I knew this was true, but it didn't seem true enough. Jimmy's gaze was guarded but deep, and his eyes had gone ugly.

While we waited Oscar crouched, handling one of the shovels.

"You know, David, it takes a long time before you get a feel for putting an edge on things."

I agreed easily, for the shovel he chose was one I had reworked. Oscar drew his thumb across the fresh steel. Then he knelt, picked up my file, and with even strokes worked his way around the blade. He handed me the shovel when he was done.

"Or maybe it's like a woman." He looked past the flat and seemed to watch a special picture form around the word. "You don't really know how to treat her until you find out what she can do for you, the kind of difference she can make." He smiled, as though surprised at himself, and walked away with Speyer toward the mess hall.

I had seen Oscar only once before, at the beginning of fire school, and I was surprised he knew my name. Like heroes, district rangers come large. Although Oscar could not have been more than five-six, no one ever thought him small. He tended his district like a farm ten generations in the family. Oscar held the land in trust, translating shuffles in federal policy on the land's behalf. He was, I suppose, everything the Forest Service or Walt Disney would have us believe about rangers. The American dirge swells with ideals that became clichés we no longer believe in. Rangers now are mostly career men in the thinnest sense of that term. The ground they covet is the beaten path that leads to the supervisor's office; with luck, the regional office or even Washington. Oscar never wanted to be anything but a field ranger.

Between Oscar and Cable, the distance was charred. This had been plain at fire school. Oscar was civil and correct with Cable, using a sector of his personality he clearly wasn't comfortable with. Oscar had a reverence for all that grew and suffered Cable as a mercenary, necessary to match the plundering fire. Cable glowed only against the fire, did not try to pretend otherwise, and responded with the license and contempt of a hired gun. Their common work was like a family bond; their enmity must have taken on some of the pain of standing against your own blood. The times I saw them together, neither diminished in the other's presence. Oscar didn't stay for supper.

After we ate, back in the barracks, Mundeen collected the crew and explained his rating system. It ran from coxman apprentice through golden coxman, with one honorary category.

"Now we got to figure all the cutters for at least coxman first class, except for Cominsky here. Anybody who's walked the plank with a preacher gets retired to coxman emeritus. But the farmers, now there's a pretty sorry bunch of dudes. You've got Moya at second class and maybe Brigham Orem—can't smoke, can't drink, can't dance; what else can he do with them? He must have dipped his wick in the cookie jar once or twice."

Laughter broke around Orem and I was glad that attention had shifted. Kruger and Snead were crowding me on either side, but as I started to ease away they grabbed me. I struggled, then decided to stay loose and get it over with. Although I had seen Mundeen work some of his pain inflictors— the patella pat, the sideburn ripaway twist, the de-archer— he had given me only the clavicle crunch, standard initiation for all new scrapers. Mike claimed he'd learned most of his repertoire from offensive linemen he'd played against. Linebackers, he said, were animals, and defensive backs were kamikaze, but it was those offensive guards and tackles, working at the bottom of pile-ups, who knew how to really make you hurt. The names, however, were Mundeen's own touch. Still, I hadn't seen anything I couldn't handle.

But I fought again, instinctively, as Mundeen signalled and Perez began to strip off my pants. Kruger wrenched my arm viciously behind me as Perez got my shorts off. Then Mundeen cinched a short length of parachute cord around my prick and held the line taut as he tied one of his barbells to the other end. Forced up on a chair and blindfolded with a bandana—enraged, helpless, afraid—I swore at Mundeen. Then Moya produced a Playboy centerfold and Snead yanked up the bandana.

"The Grand Coxman is not without charity. Look at this and become firm." Beyond the magazine, at the back of the room, Jimmy motioned to me. Hooting and cheering, no one else saw as he held up a bowed leather lace in one hand, slit it quickly with a knife, and nodded toward me. Blindfolded again, now gripping the barbell Mundeen had thrust into my hands, I understood Jimmy's gesture.

"He who leaves the chair is no coxman. He who has really fucked is stronger than steel."

I trusted Jimmy as they pried my fingers from the barbell; stayed on the chair when the weight fell free. Jimmy was right. Mundeen had cut the cord while Snead kept tension on the line.

Mike stood amazed while most of the crew cheered.

"Christ, Service, nobody stays on the chair. I'll have to make you an honorary cutter." Mundeen wheeled. "All right you suckers, who told him?"

"Farmers are the best," said Moya, turning it into a chant and dancing around Mundeen and the chair.

"What the hell," said Mundeen, losing interest. He went over and rummaged in a bag under his bunk. "Congratulations." He tossed me a pack of Trojans as the crew whistled and clapped. "A forty thousand mile guarantee; you can run it up a road full of teeth with no flats."

Later, Mike said he was sorry it turned out to be me, but he'd told Kruger how they did it to someone last summer and Kruger had been pressing him about it. It was easier to hold Kruger responsible. There was a playfulness to Mundeen's bullying, a wit to it; unable to mimic the form, Kruger had only the content of a sadist. I told Mike it was OK, but I wasn't interested in promotion to the next rank of coxman. And I promised myself I would even things with Kruger when I got the chance.

The next day, Jimmy shrugged away my thanks for his signal. He said that trials should offer the chance for success as well as humiliation. Although the outcome had given me stature with the crew, I still winced at the stripping, especially at the direct watching of Speyer who had come in to lean in the doorway behind Jimmy.

We went through the rest of the two week shift without a fire. The time, though, was livened by the assimilation of Speyer into the crew. He seemed in his late thirties, but I never did find out how old he really was. Kruger asked about his face, and he said that years ago, before he understood about fire, he had made a mistake and been burned.

Sunday, the day after he arrived, we cut our weekly practice line. Cable started him at hook and said he would move him around until he settled into the right tool. From the first, Speyer wielded a brush hook with elegance and precision, as though it were a baton, conducting the disorder of brush into the symphonic clarity of a line. When we finished that morning, Speyer was fourth hook, bumping Cavenaugh to lead pulaski.

At first, I didn't have much to do with Speyer. He was cordial enough, but private, and the only person he talked to much was Calendar. They ate together and paired off again in the evening, often coming back to the barracks long after dark. Speyer was liked and respected by the crew, and quickly established himself, like Jimmy, beyond the range of Mundeen's marauding. Two things became quickly clear. He was scrupulously clean—more obsessive about it even than Orem. His hands were uncallused, and he tended them like surgical instruments. His work clothes were always crisp; even his car, a white Fiat, was immaculate. And he was the most gentle man I have ever known.

A few days after Speyer came, Cable ordered a snake hunt. We had killed only one random diamondback so far and Cable wanted more. He kept a snake board in the mess hall that went back fourteen seasons. Stapled to it were rattles of the diamondbacks killed each year. One season there had been thirty-seven, the largest with twenty-four rattles. Last year the crew got only eight.

The snakes moved into the open as the day cooled toward evening. We went out after supper carrying McLeods. Whoever spotted a snake had kill rights and could take the skin after if he wanted. The carcass went in Bailey's freezer until there were enough for a snake fry.

When a hunter found a snake, he would circle behind it while his partner rustled around as a distraction. When the first man was in position, his partner would thrust his McLeod forward, forcing a strike. As the snake recoiled, the hunter would bring down his McLeod, severing the body. It was considered bad form to ruin the skin by slicing very far behind the head. And no prodder ever collected ten dollars from Cable by checking the reflex that jerked you back when the fangs clanged against your goading McLeod.

Jimmy would not go on the hunts. Speyer went, once. Just at dusk, Calendar, Speyer, and Perez stirred up a snake. Some of us dropped down the gully to watch as Calendar circled behind it. He signalled and Speyer moved in, McLeod extended. The diamondback struck, and in the late light I couldn't see Speyer flinch when the fangs rang against the metal. What he had done, though, with stunning speed, was embed the McLeod's prongs in the ground, pinning the snake between two prongs. Buzzing in frenzy, the snake wrenched its head up trying to strike, its body lashing the ground. Speyer watched Calendar who had taken a stumbling, reflexive step back. Calendar shook his head.

"He's yours."

Speyer scanned the rest of us, then glanced back at Perez. Released, the snake curled quickly into the brush. A trickle of venom had thickened on the face of the McLeod. Speyer wiped the tool in the dirt. No one ever said anything to Cable.

Speyer did a splendid thing with a lizard, too, that confirmed his gentleness with living things. Several days after the hunt, during breaks and after lunch, he began feeding the blue lizards bits of bacon. Before, the lizards had served only as small entertainment. When one would go immobile at the end of a darting scurry, we would lob small rocks trying to stun it. Speyer soon concentrated on one bold lizard, and by the end of the week he had us as an audience. Sitting on the barracks steps, he would lay his hand, palm up, on the ground. He set bacon pieces in it, placing more in the crook of his arm and on his shoulder. The lizard would come from under the steps, moving quickly, then stopping to do a sort of push-up and pant in its throat like a frog. It took the food in his palm, then ran easily up to his elbow and finally all the way to his shoulder. After a few days, Moya and Pitkin, who were the most enthusiastic, pressed Speyer to expand his performance. Speyer seemed oddly uneasy with Pitkin, but was bantered into it by Moya. During afternoon break, he repeated the usual sequence. But this time, when the lizard had eaten from his shoulder, Speyer slowly turned his face to it, mouth open. Tensed to run, the lizard suddenly thrust its upper body inside Speyer's mouth. It came out with a shred of bacon, then flashed down his arm and out of sight. A quick current passed. Pitkin seemed stunned, but the rest of us pressed our amazement and praise on Speyer. Mundeen, who had heard about the snake, said Speyer should start a reptile ranch. Speyer smiled and said he wasn't sure there was much future in it.

The next day, Stinson found the lizard dead, slit open, its guts spread out triangular on a rock.

Later that morning we cut practice line. We were working with a new technique, and I was up front throwing brush for the hooks. I had dropped back to retie my boots when I saw Jimmy miss his footing and stumble into Speyer. Jimmy jumped away electrically and spun, pointing his hook. Speyer watched him evenly. Jimmy said something quickly, in Spanish I thought, and turned back to work. Speyer made a small gesture of puzzlement at me and began cutting again.

That evening I sat with Jimmy while he worked grease into his boots. To the northwest, the high domes of the Santa Sangres still held the sun. Closer, plumes of yucca rose like adorned phalluses, erupting from the level monotony of brush. It was the kind of time when you either said nothing at all or what you needed to. I wanted to ask Jimmy about Speyer and finally I did.

After a while he said "I know him."

"Know him, Speyer? From where?"

"I know him," he said, and touched his buckle with the palm of his hand. "Here."

He began to relace his boots.

"What did you say on the line today? To Speyer."

"That I had no wish to run into him."

From the beginning Jimmy hated Speyer, beyond reason and without explanation. I have seen hate since, but it has always been able, even eager, to explain itself. Jimmy would say nothing about it at first; later, his references to Speyer were so oblique and fantastic that I could never be certain it was Speyer he spoke of.

Hate that roots like that in a man can break a crew. Sides are chosen, and each man withdraws to the private circle he stepped out of to form the larger perimeter of a crew. I think Jimmy's hate, unrelieved, would have broken Dalton, disassembling the whole into fractions, rendering us a collection of men, not a crew. Maybe Cable could have stopped it, but I don't think so.

But one Monday, two days before our weekend, summer finished kindling and came in hard. The hills went tinder brown and the burning index was critical. Standby was extended from six in the morning to ten at night. Thursday we rolled.

For five weeks we rolled almost every day we weren't already on the line. The low and middle canyons of the Santa Sangres no longer filled with early haze that dissolved in the sun. In its place, ochre smoke stung in the air, the sun a swollen lobe behind it. We came to measure time by shifts, distance in chains of line, and counted as pleasure anything that didn't hurt. Green Peter, Cripple, Arroyo Seco, Ten Mile, Ding Dong. Four hotshot crews and too much fire. Scree, Rib Ridge, Schoolhouse, Cargo Creek. They brought in men. Recruits from Fort Ord who complained of the heat, drank too much water, and cramped on the line. Convicts who worked as hard as men paid forty cents an hour are likely to. Pickup crews from the field towns of the San Joaquin valley who hid in the brush, drank tokay, broke their tools, and slept. Rincon, Captain Prairie, Fishhook. We learned to cut line, balanced on the fatal edge of fatigue. We cut while sweat turned the ash and dirt on our faces to mud and wore calluses over our blisters. Dirty, brutal, deadly work.

I learned about fire in those weeks. How a yucca base would burn through and vault down a slope, strewing embers across your line. The way a ridge could pre-heat, vapors driven from its oily brush, and explode with the sound of a jet lifting off and heat you could feel half a mile away. I watched rabbits, their fur ablaze, in a blind death dash away from the fire. Fire that quit when it had no reason to and burned against all odds; fire that took only ground cover, then wheeled back through the scorched canopy like wind through barbed wire.

I learned from Jimmy too, in pieces here and there. He refined me with casual suggestions—teaching me the small things that help a man hold together on the line. And I needed the help. At lead shovel, I was often on the verge of being in over my head physically. I couldn't overpower my position; Jimmy showed me how to compensate with technique. I learned to wear two pair of socks and carry extra gloves inside my shirt. I stopped using the vulnerable bow, cinching my boots instead with a double square knot. I had tried gum, sour candy, rocks, anything to suck against thirst. We carried two quart canteens on our pistol belt to replace what we sweated, not to indulge thirst. Jimmy taught me how bitterbrush leaves moistened cottonmouth, the trick of mouthing water and spitting it back in the canteen, and best, the quenching of green oranges. He showed me, too, how to protect my headlamp cord from tangling brush by running the cord inside the back of my fireshirt, looping it once around my belt, and connecting it to a battery inside a canteen pouch on my pistol belt.

The headlamp tutoring was especially useful, for we often worked at night. Unless we were initial attack crew or conditions were promising for quick containment, the Forest Service held out its hotshot crews during the day. Instead, they paraded the convict and pickup crews in great numbers up and down the line for the newspaper photographers. Television cameramen shot dramatic footage in time for the six o'clock new—often of aerial retardant drops or ground tankers pouring water to accessible parts of the fire. Then, with the lowering winds and temperature and higher humidity, the hotshot crews moved out at dusk and cut line through the night. The fires, largely, were won or lost then.

The run of fires quit after five weeks. We had held the largest to less than eight hundred acres. Cable seemed satisfied that we had tempered into a crew and eased off on training. We, too, felt tough and confident. Deep into July, the season seemed mature and we had proven capable, more than its match. Cable must have known the summer could erupt beyond anything we had yet cut against. I suppose Speyer and maybe Cominsky did too. But it was only Jimmy, wedging himself against our poise, whose presence suggested that what had passed was preface.

IV

Rounding into August, the hills tinted green with small, unseasonal rain, we entrenched into garrison life. Time slowed and strung itself out, especially after supper. We played poker and pinochle until everybody seemed to run out of money. Stonecrofter, gaseous from the junk food that filled three shelves in his locker, won the fart lighting contest, but forfeited this minor improvement in his standing on the crew by shrieking when Kruger popped a bag behind him just as he ignited a rumbler of the first magnitude. Strength was a luxury now and we indulged it, trying each other in arm-wrestling, obstacle course time, weight lifting. Some challenged Cable at one-arm push-ups, but only Snead could do as many as half of Cable's ten. I saw Kelly when I could, and started smoking a little again. The intervals in town were about right for me: I was greedy for the sex, and prepared for Kelly's increasingly pointed assumptions about our future.

Our days dulled into scuffles with monotony and laboring routine. Cable resented the Forest Service puttering ethic that filled such time with makeshift project work. We rearranged large rocks in campgrounds to make them appear more natural, pruned and planted trees along nature walks, replaced wooden trail markers with metal plaques. Cable said the government could fuck itself, and made no demands of us in such tinkering except to look busy. While we lagged through the day's job, he stayed in the truck by the radio, waiting for fire traffic, memorizing the intricate fire control maps of Southern California forests.

We still cut practice line each Sunday, and here Cable permitted no slackening. One Sunday, though, after camp chores, Cable gathered us in the mess hall. We were glad enough to have the line cutting postponed, but Moya spoke our fear that postponement only concealed less pleasant work. Cable was at a table going through a pile of papers. I noticed a lot of unopened envelopes in the stack. His mouth lapsed into a grin as Moya spoke.

"Hey, Mr. Cable, I been thinking; maybe I could just go cut line by myself. That way you'd have plenty of guys for whatever might come up, you know?"

"I'd hate to see you outsmart yourself and get stuck with some work for a change."

"Just like you said, Mr. Cable." Moya snapped his fingers. "You and me, we can take care of it. The rest of these suckers can cut line." Cable looked up now. His face still held traces of the grin. We shuffled into silence.

"Yesterday I got some stuff from the forest supervisor. What's happened is the Regional Office set up a special award and we're in line for it."

Mundeen moaned and rumbled "Here comes the gas."

"I change my mind back, Mr. Cable."

"OK, listen up now." But the bantering stayed in his voice. "The RO has checked out the performance records of all the hotshot crews in the region for July. It turns out we're tied with China Hat"—he spoke through a few hoots— "for top crew in the region. Since we're both on the same Forest, they left it up to the supervisor." He stopped, dangling prospects before us. "And it looks like we're going to have some kind of face-off to settle it."

This time he had to stop altogether as we howled and stomped our pleasure. China Hat was thought to be a favorite of the forest supervisor. Stocked largely with forestry majors—planters, Cable called them—they were often featured in news releases put out by the public information officer. They had new equipment a season or two before we or Chilao got it, and they seemed to get first shot at the lucrative, out-of-state fires. We had seen them on the line a few times. They were good; we were better.

When we had settled a little, Cable explained the terms of the match. The SO had set up four individual and four crew events. The individual duels would involve each of the line tools. Crew competition would require a two mile run, an assortment of pt exercises, a written exam on the Health and Safety Code and Fireline Handbook, and, at the end, a one hour line cut. We would meet them next Sunday.

Cable took us out then for a one hour line cut, rehearsing us to explode our measured, durable pace into a sprint. That afternoon, and each morning for the rest of the week, we studied sections of the Forest Service manuals. We traded the obstacle course for a daily three mile run, and in the evenings four of us worked out for the individual competition. Cable had picked Jimmy and Cavenaugh for brush hook and pulaski. Orem was our McLeod. And I would be going at shovel. Jimmy, who wouldn't use his line hook even in Sunday practice, did little in preparation except to hone the project hook he'd be cutting with. As lead pulaski, Cavenaugh used the tool like an ax. He practiced now with Cominsky, learning the uses of the grubbing head. Orem experimented with a shorthandled McLeod, and I concentrated on hurling loads of dirt for volume, accuracy, and distance.

As we moved through the week, the camp took on the feel of a carnival. At night, in the barracks, Moya got out his guitar and we improvised lyrics to Smokey the Bear, ridiculing China Hat and predicting their ruin in the competition. Jarvis, a fan of Bob Dylan, taught Moya the chords to "Oxford Town" and we added to our playlist "Newhall Town, Newhall Town/ Fire a-burnin' all around/ China Hat been shut down/ Dalton goin' down to Newhall Town." We drilled each other on the Fireline Handbook and levied a fine for every wrong answer. Even Cable got caught up, complaining that no match had been arranged between him and the China Hat superintendent.

Though the carnival pitch was dominant, it was not unanimous. Jimmy took no part in it. He might have disapproved of the whole affair, but indifference and disapproval were hard to sort out in him. Speyer, who read through much of his free time, seemed mildly amused by our enthusiasm. He mattered little to our mood, though, for he had a knack for invisibility, never seeming to be there unless you specifically looked for him. But Perez and Snead mattered, and both were sour at not being picked for pulaski. Perez was especially sullen, talking now only to Calendar, grudging and slacking off in our practice line cuts. One night near the end of the week, he finally called Cavenaugh on it. We had just finished a round of questions on backfiring that cost Perez a dollar. He threw a handful of change across the room at the fine box and the coins ricocheted off the wall.

"I don't have to learn that shit."

"Sure," said Moya. "You're a big shot."

"Cram it up your mouth. I ain't gonna take no more shit, not from anybody, not even from you." Then it came. "Nobody on this fucking crew can swing a pulaski better than me. Not nobody." He challenged Cavenaugh with a straight-on look.

"Could be," said Cavenaugh, stretched out on his bunk with a copy of *Playboy*. Cable doesn't seem to think so."

"Yeah, and what do you think?" Perez rolled one shoulder a little, as if loosening a kink.

"I think if you don't like it you know where I live."

"Me too," said Mundeen, rocking off his bunk. "What kind of shit you trying to pull, Perez?"

"Fuck you lard ass. I want any shit from you, I'll squeeze your head. I can take you both."

Mundeen motioned with his hands. "Well let it come, greaser."

"No more!" The authority in the voice iced the room into a tableau. Jimmy came down the bunks, ablaze.

"You!" he said to Perez. There was a moment when anything could have happened. Then Perez spit on the floor, spun away, and walked out.

In the uneasy run of talk that followed, someone said that Perez was pretty good, but not that good.

"He could be Genghis Khan with a pulaski and it wouldn't do him any good." Calendar spoke to the rest of us so seldom that we listened. "He's not going at pulaski for the same reason the man jumped Orem over Moya. Cable wants to win, but he wants to win white."

"Bullshit," said Moya. "This ain't no civil rights march. Besides," he glinted, "Supermouse taught Orem everything he knows. He's my boy."

Calendar shook out a cigarette and lit it. "Play it his way, then."

It blunted our edge for the night, but we came back keen the next morning. After breakfast, Cable gave us a quiz on the helitack section of the Handbook. The two best scores would ride into Arcadia with Cominsky to pick up supplies at the forest warehouse. Calendar and I didn't miss a question. After the morning run, Cominsky warmed up the old stakeside. We settled into the back, and as we wheeled out of the yard I flipped a cheerful finger to Mundeen who was starting to wash the mess hall windows.

When we reached the pavement, Calendar took a paperback from his pocket, read a little, then put it down. We both watched the country for a while until the road buttonhooked into the freeway. The book began to ruffle in the wind, and Calendar picked it up.

"Ever read Díaz Soto y Gama?"

I shook my head. "What's he done?"

Calendar slid the book back in his jeans, then got out a cigarette and hunched into the air pocket behind the cab to light it.

"He established the theoretical basis for the Mexican Revolution. Carranza wanted him for minister of justice, but he saw through that. Carranza just wanted him in Mexico City where they could keep an eye on him."

"I guess I don't know much about that."

"Why should you?" He pulled at the cigarette but it had gone out. "Americans think history is George Washington being hauled across some river while the band plays Yankee Doodle. The ruling class knows that history is whatever lie you want to invent, as long as you can sell it. It's one of the slickest lies they've managed to pull off."

"Oh?"

His face stiffened.

"It doesn't really matter whether you believe it. Most people are politically illiterate. And they can't be educated in this structure because they're drugged on it. Democracy is the opiate of Western Capitalism. But someday, maybe soon, it won't be a matter of believing or not believing. Things will be cleared away; then people can see what's true."

I knew enough to let that go. "Maybe I'll take a look at Soto y Gama when you're through with him."

"You read Spanish?"

"No."

He ducked again and scratched another wooden match. "I don't think you'd get much out of him anyway."

On the way back, I asked why he'd taken notes at fire school. When he answered, his voice seemed off-key, as if he were coercing nonchalance from it. I noticed because I couldn't think of any reason for it.

"I guess I've always been a good student."

That night, the barracks seethed again with anticipation of Sunday. Stinson was drilling Pitkin on the chain of command on a project fire. Dick, who had trouble remembering his phone number, worked hard at the lesson around volleys of diversion.

"OK, the last time now. Who works for the line boss?"

"The division boss."

"Right. . . ."

"And the line scout, and the tanker boss, and the tractor boss. . . ." Pitkin paused, repeated "tractor boss," then faltered, his sequence broken. Moya began to strum "Old McDonald."

"And the airplane boss."

"Air attack boss."

Moya switched to "Eight Miles High" and chipped in singing falsetto. Flustering, Pitkin rushed on.

"The, uh, section boss. Not, not him."

He was trying so hard several of us looked away, embarrassed, as if we were watching a cripple trying to maneuver his vacant body. Moya waited now in sympathetic silence, but Kruger, on his way to the showers imitating Dick's bow-legged walk, kept at him.

"Hey, Pits, when they ask for your name on that test, see if you can't pull down fifty percent."

"I'll do all right. You'll see. Mr. Cable is counting on me."

"No kidding?" Kruger pretended great relief. "That wraps Sunday up bigger than shit. Maybe you're right; when you show up China Hat's gonna be laughing too hard to do anything."

"Fuck off," said Moya.

Kruger let out a serrated laugh. "You fuck with the bull, Mouse, you likely to get the horns."

Moya answered in Spanish, then broke into rollicking laughter.

"You can talk spic till it's coming out your ears. You got something to say to me, you can talk like a white man."

"Kruger! Where's that fucking soap!" Mundeen roared and echoed from the showers.

Kruger turned away. Moya strummed an ear-grating cord after him.

After a while I went over to the mess hall. Sometimes Bailey would put out leftovers before locking the kitchen where he washed up, listening to the drone of talk shows on his perpetual radio. Mundeen said he kept it on all night. Stonecrofter and Cominsky were finishing the last pieces of pie when I came in. I had some coffee with them and went out to the truck to change the water in my canteens.

A light wind rattled the hooded scrub oak, carrying pieces of laughter away from the barracks. The great bulk of the Santa Sangres crowded the northern sky, but south and west above the ridge the night opened cleanly onto final distances. The balance of things shifted a fraction and poised, perfectly still, in multiple equilibrium. And shifted again as I swung up on the truck and found Jimmy. He was sitting near the cab, rigid, knees together. His hands were pressed flat on his thighs. I said his name twice before he let out a slow breath, slumped, and turned to see me.

"David," he said, as if acknowledging something. He seemed to be coming back from a long way.

"Are you all right?"

"I am all right," he said, back all the way now.

"Was something wrong?"

"I am all right," he said again. "Do what it was you came for and I will rest to myself a little. We can talk then."

I started to work my canteens out of their pouches and realized I had come alert against making noise. I took the canteens across to the faucet outside the tool shed, circling at the last moment the lighted perimeter of the mess hall. When I was done I held myself, squatting by the dripping faucet, until what seemed like enough time had passed. Noise from the barracks swelled as I came back, feeling like a fugitive, uneasy in the feeling, puzzled that I was acting like one.

I put away the canteens without saying anything. Jimmy was finishing a cigarette, holding it backwards under the cup of his palm. He pressed it out on his boot sole and dropped the butt in his pocket.

"So it has become time now for us to talk." His hand drifted to his buckle. The silver surfaced in the dark as though it were lit with a dull, inner glow. "I know some things and I will tell you some truth about them. About fire most. Because no one else is here for you. I must listen also to how I say these things."

He withdrew into long silence and I disciplined myself against breaking it. When he began again, the pitch of his voice was higher and it carried the seal of command I had heard in the barracks the night before. The language and syntax were peculiar; the cadence, archaic. Jimmy's English was Spartan but serviceable. This was wholly different. It could have been a trick of the wind, but it seemed as though his words hardly carried beyond me, draining away in the air behind my head.

"You see the fire die under your shovel; against your strength, ashes. You believe this is an ending. Cut a thistle, it grows itself again ten times. Fire makes all its pieces and is made back out of them. It must burn again and again to be strong, to live even. We know its pieces only.

And we are pieces only, part of which God that bears us, and even when we die the God goes on. But one day maybe there is need for the God to draw all his pieces to him and risk everything and if he loses he is finished and all his parts. Yes. And with fire also."

"Now you must hear it and I will tell you and perhaps the God that carries you in his belly will let you to understand. Listen: time ago fifteen years, for which I do not understand, fire became whole, one thing. Once it was a final thing, world made of fire, forever, with no need. But that time, back before first man even, it warred with earth and water and lost. Lost almost everything. And then it must wait a long time for man and then it must wait a long time still and when it could make sex again with wind it came and that was time ago fifteen years. It burned up Cable's arm and what you call soul, it burned up my brother and other men, it burned on long hills and long canyons. But it gave a mistake about our strength and it lost courage at one important place. We could not finish the whole. The whole escaped away from us. And it has healed itself; it is strong again now, white and yellow and blue. Its doom runners come already before it. Whose name cannot be said prepares its way. And it must be soon for we grow in strength and one day, maybe already, it weaks fire more to make pieces than it claws strength back from them. It must come soon or it loses all chance. And I will know it coming. Its smell and the look of its burning; it has printed my blood and I will know it. It will burn up all people. Or it will be scattered and made cold always. And if it is dead there can be fires still but they will mean nothing. They will wander on the hills for no reason and their power will die at the end of their tongues and feed no mouth."

"I know this, and I have been given a little of how to understand about it. There are others. Things happen to Cable he does not know about. He pretends he feels nothing, believes he has bad dreams. He does not trust the eye's corner, but he gets ready now a little right and left. And the cloudless child, all things possible to him, each thing marking him. That is enough."

A welling of wonder and confusion swarmed in me against any speaking. It settled finally in one question whose source I could not trace but did not doubt.

"Speyer. Is that why, I mean, does he. . .have something to do with this?"

"That is only my matter." Jimmy's voice was flat and familiar again. And one more question, coming from a sense of flattery and uneasiness.

"Why did you tell me this?"

"You must answer for yourself."

When I left the truck, Jimmy had not moved except to hug himself against the rippling chill that had ridden into the wind.

The next morning was Saturday. Cable worked us lightly in pt, then had us clean our gear and the truck. I waited until Jimmy was alone. The color in his face seemed to have collected in a dark flush just under the skin. I tried to seem casual but I felt awkward, guilty, as though an ugly secret had been forced on me— a secret that would pollute me unless I understood it whole. I had thought a long time in the dark in my bunk, my mind eddying back when I tried to swim free into sleep. After breakfast I asked Cominsky again about Cable's arm. He said Cable had told him what happened, and besides his cousin had been in Cable's company in Korea. It seemed a firm enough place to begin.

When I asked, Jimmy shrugged and looked back to waxing his hook's handle.

"Here, Korea, it does not matter. You heard only what you listened for."

That night I shored myself against the crest of our rush toward Sunday. It didn't come. Instead, most of the crew drifted into themselves and the lights were out by ten.

We had breakfast an hour early the next morning, then hunkered down for the cold ride to the China Hat station. Oscar was there ahead of us, along with the Newhall district ranger and Turpin, the fire control officer for the Forest. The China Hat superintendent, a beefy and cordial young man on his way up in fire control, came out to meet Cable as he swung down from the cab. Cable told us to unload and loosen up, then went inside with the rest of the overhead. The China Hat crew lounged in the sun at the side of the mess hall, appraising us as we got down. We stood by the truck, moving our legs against the stiffness that came from the chilly ride, forcing a little talk to ease the foolishness of standing there on display with nothing to do. Someone from China Hat rolled a long wolf whistle. Mundeen, a little apart up front, leaned back on his elbows against the cab.

"They must be whistling at themselves. That's the only pussy I see around here."

"See, I told you guys. Dalton hires beef so dumb they can't figure out what they see when they look in the mirror. The Dalton Longshots."

Mundeen and the China Hat man were looking at each other now, but it was Moya who answered.

"We're so good we can put it in Mexican overdrive and whistle all the way."

"Yeah," said Stinson, "just drop it in neutral and coast on home."

"You're gonna have to." The China Hat man grinned his challenge. "You won't have enough gas for a fart when we're through with you."

"We're the best in the West," piped Pitkin. Dick's fingers skittered against each other, as though he were trying to pick something off them.

"Mother, I heard Dalton was hard up, but I didn't know things were this bad." A second China Hat man pretended to speak to his friends, but cast his voice far enough to reach us. "Quick, nurse, it's Ricky Retardo doing nursery rhymes. Who tied your shoelaces for you this morning, Ricky?"

Pitkin looked down at his boots.

"Back off," said Mundeen, no longer leaning.

"And the fat man thinks he's Smokey the Badass. Save me, nurse."

"You want to find out something?" Mundeen moved now, slowly but without hesitation, toward the cluster of China Hat crewmen.

The mess hall door banged and Cable was on the top step. He stood there long enough to scan both crews, then came down, got his clipboard from the truck, and went back in. Cominsky got out his pulaski and began filing it. Others followed and China Hat drifted back to talk among themselves. Then one of them called across to us again.

"Pete, hey, Jarvis."

Jarvis looked up from his filing.

"Remmy, no kidding. I didn't know you were down here." He got up and started walking over. He was almost there when Kruger called after him, mimicking the other voice.

"Ranger, hey, Jarv ass. You best watch who you hang out with if you want to live long enough to grow up to be Smokey the Bear."

Jarvis spun around, but then just said "We go to school together."

"Hey, Mike, hear that? They're gonna be a cinch. I bet they got two or three more midgets from Stump State." Glee got into his voice at this cleverness. "What'd they get, two or three first downs on us last year? Let's hear it for Humble State." Kruger was winding now, having rehearsed all this on Jarvis when he discovered that Pete came from Humboldt State.

Most of the China Hat crew were looking at Kruger, but no one answered him.

"Shit," said Kruger, and turned away.

The overhead came out and we went up to where courses had been set for the individual competitions. They would start with the hooks, and move back through the cutting order. The line the hooks would cut had been marked in blue ribbon through a manzanita thicket. They had half an hour to cut as far and cleanly as they could. Ray, the hook cutting against Jimmy, was built on the dimensions of Mundeen but a little shorter. He was the one who had taunted us first; to beat him would mean a lot.

At the start he muscled into the tangle of springy stems, overpowering them with a churning swing. Jimmy's motions seemed flimsy in comparison, but at each swing a branch shuddered and let go. After twenty minutes Jimmy had moved well ahead and Ray was pressing all the way now, losing whatever finesse he had, swearing when the manzanita flexed away intact from his hook or sagged back into the snarly growth, slit but not cut through. He began to nick his blade on rocks as he lost control after wild swings. Then Jimmy slowed, and at the end was no more than a few yards ahead. He wasn't tired; I could see that from his almost even breathing; he had just eased off and Ray had come close enough to repair the dent in China Hat's confidence.

As we moved to the pulaski course, I walked behind Jimmy and Pitkin. Dick asked why he didn't try harder. I got just a piece of Jimmy's low, short answer.

"Like children. . .less to ask pardon of."

The terrain at the pulaski course was more open with a few sapling pines, some scrub oak, and sage for ground cover. From the start, it was clear Cavenaugh would win. He was stronger, and the precision of his cuts made all his strength count. Even his work with the grubbing blade was better. We had ten points now, and momentum.

The shovel competition was broken into three parts. The China Hat shovel, a redhead called Sparky, was rangily muscled like a hook. He beat me cleanly at the scraping, leaning into the work as if his back had no nerves. He was strong enough to use only his arms and shoulders, while I braced my forearm along my thigh and pivoted around with each sweep, driving with my leg, supplementing and saving arm strength, losing ground. In the dirt throw for volume and distance, I reached back to reserves I'd assembled all summer. When Turpin weighed the two lines of buckets, mine were heavier. The last event measured height and accuracy, simulating the times on the line when a shovel must loft dirt into trees, trying to muffle the flames before they crown out. We had five minutes to get what dirt we could into buckets hung from a line thirty feet from the ground and twenty from where we stood. To reach mine, I had to cut back to less than half a shovel load. Sparky was able to throw nearly a full load. He lost what seemed a lot of dirt in his scattering throw, but he was throwing with good speed and some of my compact loads dropped wide of the bucket. I knew I was beaten even before they lowered and weighed the buckets.

Sweat had dripped on my glasses, making muddy streaks on the dust-filmed lens. While I was cleaning them, Mundeen came over and said Sparky had more even ground on the scraping course. It didn't help much.

In the McLeod match, Orem had started fast and was well ahead by the time I had my glasses back on. He looked good, rocking his body into each reach, pulling with his shoulders instead of his arms. But he was breathing hard already, moving at a pace he couldn't sustain. The China Hat McLeod plowed away without much skill, but powerfully. As they moved into the last length of the course, Orem slowed and the China Hat man closed in a driving sprint. But he had started too cautiously, giving away too much, and although he was still making up ground at the end, Orem hung on, tight as a miler in the stretch, to cross the finish first. Orem grabbed his thigh and went down, rocking on the ground against a cramp. Turpin walked the two lines, comparing their caliber. Then he talked to Cable and the China Hat sup. Cable swung away from them in an anger-stiff walk and came back to where we were grouped around Orem. Turpin had given China Hat the win. We broke for lunch, even in points.

After we ate, Turpin passed out the written test. Although we had worked hard on the Fireline Handbook, we had conceded this part of the competition. China Hat was nearly an all-college crew, and we had three or four men whose high school grades had been kept above water by shop, P. E., and study hall. Pitkin would be hopelessly lost.

But we won it, even after a recount of scores, and China Hat was shaken. In the pt test that followed, even with some disqualifications for doubtful violations in push-ups and squat thrusts, we picked up twenty more points. Now China Hat had to win both the run and the line cut just to tie us. Moya won the two mile easily, we took six of the first nine places, and four China Hat men, including Ray and Sparky, slowed almost to a walk the last quarter mile, talking to each other as they jogged in, losing even to Stonecrofter and Cominsky. Turpin cancelled the line cut. Later in the summer, a directive from the regional office prohibited any further intercrew matches.

We loaded up while Cable went in for a last cup of coffee. Oscar congratulated us and went in too. Most of the China Hat crew had disappeared, but Ray, Sparky, and one other man were standing near the corner of the mess hall, passing around a canteen. Ray spit a mouthful of water into the dirt.

"Hey, Mundeen, we're gonna get your ass this fall."

Mundeen muscled around on the seat and looked at him. "You that wimpy guard I kept knocking over on sweeps last year?"

"Your ass, Mundeen."

"You know where I live."

"Be looking for me."

Ray took more water and spit, but the stream came apart, splattering down his jeans. A rising and peeling whoop poured from the truck as Cable and the others came out.

Cable asked us to wait around after supper. When everyone was finished, he scraped back from the table.

"A few things. I noticed a couple of you weren't very interested in putting out today. You best work out some good excuses. I'll be wanting to hear them." I forced myself to meet Cable's scanning gaze, afraid he had seen my loss as lagging.

"And just in case anybody was thinking about leaning on Service and Orem, you might want to know they were up against China Hat's second and third hooks." The weight of losing lightened as the crew ground up the deception. Being beaten by one of their top men took away some of the sting.

"I asked our good buddy Turpin and he said there was nothing about not doing it in the rules. I should've decked the cocksucker. Anyway, tomorrow came in a six, so you've got the day off. There's gonna be a kegger up the East Fork fire spur. Any woman who'd go out with you culls is welcome. I'm buying."

For the second time that day we roared our pleasure, thumping the sound off the walls.

"And one more thing." Cable's voice filtered through our racket. "Goddamn good job."

V

After Cable cancelled standby, Mike and I drove into town together. The past two weekends I'd volunteered for some overtime, filling in at a tanker station on my days off. I was swollen with anticipation of a night with Kelly.

Karen was working a late shift at the drive-in, so the three of us sat around drinking beer, Mike and I high and lively, bragging about our match with China Hat. I managed to put the best possible construction on my loss to Sparky, emphasizing my high score on the written test and solid placement in the two mile run. Kelly didn't say much. When Karen came home, her mindless chirping, which usually registered as background noise, was a welcome distraction from Kelly's odd and increasingly sullen distance. After a few more beers, Mike and Karen went down the hall to her room. There was laughing, a shriek, and after some silence the accelerating cadence of bedsprings. I went out to the kitchen for another beer. The sound had stopped when I came back. I tried again to lighten the evening and turn it towards bed.

"I'm glad to hear I'm not the only short-timer in the house." I nodded toward their room.

Kelly had been scratching Earth's neck. She pushed him roughly away.

"Do all men screw with a stopwatch strapped to their cocks?" Her tone was even more toxic than her words. "Put're there, Mack.

Sis, boom, bah; ream that cunt. Last man down is a dildo. Did you all outfuck China Hat, or is this still part of the game?"

Kelly had dipped into quick anger before but it had never been like this, skittering on the edge of hysteria. Earth winced away at the sound and rolled on his back to be scratched.

"If you don't want to go to bed with me, just say so."

"'Just say so.' What'd that sound like, the weather forecast?" Her voice was shaking now.

I've never dealt well with being mocked. I could have asked what was really wrong, but her mimicry raised anger in me that cut off any patient instincts. I got up to go.

"That's right, hero, hit the road; the whorehouse just shut down." She was crying now, but it didn't matter. I was almost to the curb when she came out, stumbling as she ran down the steps.

"David, David please I'm sorry. I am, don't go, I really am." She kept saying "I am," arms locked around me, crying. In a shiver of detachment I felt suddenly removed from both of us, as if we were inert tokens, mechanical pieces that I could direct, without emotion, to any end. It was an ugly feeling, and it didn't go away for a while.

We went back inside, up to her room. A clutter of clothes made the room seem more intimate than before. We sat on the bed, not touching.

"Do you want to talk?"

Kelly shook her head, sniffing into a wad of Kleenex.

"OK. How about some wine?"

"Yes."

Karen came into the kitchen while I was looking for a clean glass.

"What was all that about?" She looked unraveled and a little edgy, standing just inside the doorway, squinting without her contacts. She was wearing Mike's shirt, its tails almost to her knees.

"I don't know. She hasn't said yet."

Karen kept looking at me.

"I really don't know. Do you?"

"I might." She unfolded her arms, then folded them again. "And you should."

I leaned against the counter and took a sip of beer. My stomach felt like a freefall down an elevator shaft. What if Kelly was pregnant?

"Listen, Kelly's really stuck on you. Well don't look so surprised. We've been best friends since high school and I've never seen her like this before. You're the only thing she thinks about besides those dumb cards and the last couple weeks when you didn't come in or call she'd say crazy things and act funny and run me right out of the house if I tried to say anything. Love is what's wrong, and if you can't see that you better get some new glasses."

She padded back down the hall before I could think of an answer.

When I got back the room was dark, lit only by a streetlight down the block.

"Hi there, fireman," Kelly said softly.

As my eyes settled into the faint light, I eased across the room to the bed. Kelly lay on her back, pale against the dark bedspread, her face obscure.

"You don't have to Kell, really. Not if you don't want to."

"I want to."

It was the best we'd been together.

"When you were little, did you ever think you wouldn't grow up?" Kelly was rubbing my shoulder which had stiffened since this morning. I was drinking the beer which wasn't very cold now.

"I don't know. I guess so."

"I used to think that a lot."

"Um."

Kelly reached across me for her wine, pressing ridges of rib into my back.

"And now sometimes, you know, I wish I hadn't."

"Thought that?"

"No, grown up."

I reached over and traced her nipple with my finger.

"I'm glad you did."

Kelly punched me lightly.

"You boob men. . . ."

A moth ticked against the upper window and we watched him for a while, circling away but always coming back to the same pane. He dropped to the sill finally and fluttered out.

"About tonight David, I don't know what happened to me; I don't know why I said those things."

"You sure didn't pick up 'dildo' out of *Ladies' Home Journal*."

I didn't want to talk about it. I had decided already that women wanted to talk about how things were between you, that they would crowd you beyond evasions and even silence if they could. Until you either told the truth they already knew or caved in to a lie you carried with you long after they were gone. Kelly had raked too close to the truth earlier, and it was a truth I didn't want to acknowledge. I liked her spunkiness and I liked the sex, and that was all.

"Anyway, everybody gets a little crazy now and then. No big thing." Kelly drew up her knees and stretched her arms around them.

"No, that's not true. I mean about me not knowing why I said those things." She was looking out the window again. "I've been doing the tarot on us, as many different ways as I know how, asking different questions. And it keeps on coming out the same."

"Maybe you haven't been shuffling the cards." I felt Kelly stiffen. "OK, I'm sorry. What about the tarot?"

"I knew you wouldn't believe me so I tried to make you go away. You don't want to know. You don't know anything about it so you make jokes and won't even listen."

"I'm listening now. Kelly?"

"The cards keep coming out that something outside us, something powerful and evil, something I've never seen in the tarot before, is going to rule what happens to us. And you're in terrible danger and can't see it and can't escape it unless you see. I can't help; there's nothing I can do so you've got to believe me, you've got to believe the cards." The skittery edge was back in her voice.

I believed none of it, except that Kelly thought it was true. Whatever Jimmy was, whatever he meant, his ghostwork was all I needed of shadows, and he was a lot better at it than Kelly. What he said that night in the truck kept reproducing itself in me. But I had no way to orient myself, no reference point, nothing to give me any reason to believe that either. But one havoc with Kelly was enough for the evening. I'd have to play it out.

"What kind of danger?"

"I don't know. That part's so unclear. A secret enemy, something about the color white, maybe the loss of some object. All those Wands and Swords. I know it's your job. It's something about the crew and you've got to quit or something bad, something really horrible is going to happen and I can't help it and I love you."

She rolled away from me, still hugging her knees, crying. I reached out and she turned back, hanging on, pressing her face in my shoulder.

"It's stupid, I can't help it, it's true."

The detachment came again and with it the ease of lying. The lie had nothing to do with me now; a spectator can say anything.

"I love you, Kelly Corning." And said it again and again until she was quiet.

I was almost asleep when Kelly asked, in a little voice, what I was going to do.

"Let's work that out tomorrow. Maybe you can get somebody else to read the cards."

"I did," she said, but I was too tired to answer.

We slept late the next day, then went out for breakfast with Mike and Karen. We stretched the morning out with coffee, killing time until the party. Kelly was quiet, but receptive. I felt languid and domestic. I called up the impish run of freckles on Kelly's breasts, the lunar scar on her side, and touched her under the table. Karen, who'd been trying to decide how to treat me, whether I was now properly grateful for being loved, watched Kelly nuzzle me in return.

"You know, I think you two are really paired. Mike, don't you think they're just right for each other?"

"Yumph." Mundeen was working on his second order of pancakes.

"I mean, you guys are just so obviously in tune with each other. I know, let's try an experiment. Mike, what am I thinking about?"

Mundeen looked as though someone had just asked him to name the principal export crop of Somalia.

"Whether the new diaphragm fits?"

"Mike!"

"Well, that's what you should be thinking about."

Karen got up in a pout and towed Kelly after her to the ladies' room. Mike went back to his pancakes and the sports section of the *Los Angeles Times*.

"Hey, look at this. The Rams just traded Schumacher. This horse is headed for the Coliseum."

"Is Schumacher a defensive end?"

"Second string. Jesus, I just couldn't see myself in Detroit."

"The Supremes come from Detroit."

"Yeah, so do Edsels."

After Karen and Kelly came back, the lunch rush started and the waitress stopped bringing coffee. Mike finished my hash browns and we left.

Just out of town, I blew a tire. Mike and I took turns horsing the balky jack and rusted lug nuts. We'd finished two six packs by the time we got to the turnoff for the East Fork spur. Even Kelly had a beer as the heat built toward the center of afternoon.

Kruger blew past us just before we reached the junction, fishtailing when he hit the dirt, billowing dust as he headed up the canyon. I hung back, but the dust stayed in the air a long time. I had to use the wipers as we followed Kruger's wake along the creek. About four miles up, the canyon opened into a small meadow. The remains of a wooden sign, pocked and splintered by bullets, read "Tincup Picnic Area." Beneath it on the tree was a red metal fire closure sign, shredded by buckshot. I pulled off into the meadow and parked by Jarvis. Mike grabbed Karen as she bent getting out of the car.

"Let's hit that keg. Put a little meat on your boney ass."

She slapped his hand, then made him flinch by pretending to go for his balls.

"You guys coming?"

"I'd like to go down to the creek first." Kelly looked over the hood at me. "Ok?"

"Sure."

"No grab-ass on government land," Mike said, hauling Karen after him. "Beeeer," he bellowed across the meadow and started for the keg.

Kelly and I went up the road past the meadow, then skidded down a low bank to the creek. We came out on a sand bar that must have been an island when the water was up. A hundred feet or so upstream, back to us, someone was hunched over a mound near the creek's edge. It was Pitkin. The stream noise had covered our sound coming down and he hadn't seen us. He was building a sand castle. Kelly hooked her arm through mine and we watched, not saying anything to break the small magic. When Dick finally sensed us, he looked around and lurched up, backing away from the sand castle. Kelly waved and we started up the bar. Dick looked confused and embarrassed.

"Hello, David." He brushed the sand from his hands, and his fingers kept making little motions of their own when he was done.

"Hi, Dick. This is Kelly."

"Hi." Dick ducked his head as he spoke.

"That's a nifty castle," said Kelly. "Like some help with it?"

Now Dick looked suspicious. "Well, yeah, maybe." He looked over at me. "You won't tell anybody? I mean, some of the guys. . . ."

"About our castle?" Kelly faked an aggressive "our." "He'd better not."

"No way," I said, raising my hand in pledge.

"Well, the sand here doesn't pack up like on the beach, but if you really want to. . . ."

Kelly dropped to her knees, then sat and began scooping wet sand to lengthen one wall. Dick hesitated before joining her.

"Come on, poop, pitch in."

"I'll have to sit this one out. I didn't bring my union card."

"Toad." Kelly scuffed some sand at me.

I watched for a while, then wandered away. Just above us, a rock ledge angled out from the bank, dividing the bar and ending above a nice pool. I climbed the ledge, wadded my shirt for a pillow, and stretched out. Looking across the creek, I scanned the opposite wall of the canyon, guessing how fast a fire would move on it, figuring the chances of getting a line in before the fire burned into the heavy brush higher up. It felt good to bake in the sun and sweat without working for it. Below, Dick and Kelly talked. I dozed and listened in snatches.

"If I had a girlfriend, do you think she'd like to do this? I mean, is this something girls like to do?"

"I'm a girl; I like it."

"I, I didn't mean to say it like that. . . ."

Kelly's laugh rose up, light and kind.

"I know. Don't you have a girl?"

"Well, not exactly. Not right now. You sure know how to build a real sand castle."

"I've got a good teacher. You must have made a lot of these at the beach."

"Yeah, some."

"By yourself?"

"Well, I take my cousin sometimes. She's only eight, but she likes it a lot. Sometimes I make up stories for her about who lives in the castle. I guess she likes that as much as building them."

Sweat had beaded on my chest and started to run. I rolled over and shifted on the cool rock until I was comfortable. I wondered if there were any trout in the creek. There probably weren't; the water would get too low and warm late in the summer. It would be a hard stream to fish anyway. I slipped back to sleep.

"— four years, but this time I got a real good chance."

My shoulder stung where an edge of rock had pressed into it. I sat up and rubbed the dent.

"Experience counts in your Civil Service rating and I got a lot of that. Mr. Cable told me they'd take me on full time if I passed the test. Cominsky says there's nothing to it and besides he's going to help me study up for it. It's been what I wanted ever since I first hired on. There's a lot of great guys in the Forest Service, and you got a real chance to advance yourself."

"You like the guys on the crew?"

"Sure, well. . .most of them."

I stopped rubbing my shoulder.

"It's like a family. The guys change some every season, but every year fire school is just like Christmas. It's like meeting everybody who's going to be your family that year."

"David doesn't like Kruger. I guess a lot of the crew doesn't."

"Oh, Kruger sort of picks on people but I don't pay any attention to it." Dick sounded vague and uneasy, as if he were being led toward something he didn't want but couldn't get out of.

"What about the Indian, Tommy Graystart?"

"Jimmy? Does David say things about him?" Dick's voice lurched and tightened.

"No. Just that he's a little strange."

"Well, maybe a little bit sometimes. We get along pretty good so I don't notice it. I mean we're not best friends or anything but we get along. Indians are just different, that's all. You got to make allowances."

"Who don't you get along with? David doesn't think I'm interested so he doesn't talk much about the crew. But I really am interested. It means a lot to me. Really."

The urgent pressure that had gotten into Kelly's voice puzzled me. I could think of no good reason why Dick's friends or enemies on the crew should matter much to her. And with Kruger eliminated, I didn't really want to hear his answer.

"I don't like to talk against people," Dick said slowly. Then, "Speyer."

I must have moved, because Dick turned and saw me. He looked like someone had hit him in the stomach. Dick scrambled to his feet; Kelly looked up and saw me then.

"You shit! Have you been up there all along; have you been listening to us?"

"To what? To you? All I heard was that Dick doesn't like Speyer."

"Don't tell him, don't tell anybody." Dick was really scared. "I shouldn't have said that. I didn't mean it."

Kelly got up and stood, furious, protectively in front of Dick.

"Damn you, David. Goddamn you!"

The responses seemed all out of proportion to what I said I'd heard, even to what I really had heard. As I climbed down from the rock, I decided that the tarot must be mixed up in it somehow for Kelly to be like this. Dick had no reason at all that I knew of.

"You won't, will you David? You won't tell? You got to promise you won't."

I didn't answer right away.

"You got to, you got to promise." Dick was more than scared now; he was terrified.

"Look, I don't know what's going on and I'm not going to tell anyone anything. There's nothing to tell."

"You got to promise."

"I promise," I said, a little mad now.

"I don't," said Kelly. "Not until you tell me about Speyer."

Dick looked at me. I thought he was going to cry.

"Leave him alone, Kell. She won't say anything."

"I will." Her voice was cold and absolutely level, a promise. Then her voice went gentle again, coaxing.

"David's promised and I will too. All I want to know is why you don't like Speyer. That's all. Just that and we'll never say anything." She put her hand on Dick's wrist. "Just that. Tell us that. You can tell us, Dick. Friends talk to each other, just to each other and no one else ever knows. Tell us."

She dropped to the sand, still holding Dick's wrist and pulling a little until he sat awkwardly beside her. When he started to talk he was calm, as though he were speaking about someone he hardly knew. It was eerie to listen to him.

"There's this dream, this dream I been having ever since I was a kid. It doesn't start with anything; I'm just walking along and I don't know where I'm coming from but I know I'm going someplace important. Then I start knowing my own mother's there, even though she'd been dead ever since I can remember. But I know she's there and that makes me feel the best ever. But after a while she gets too far ahead of me and I can't catch up to her and then the dream stops. I think I get a little closer to catching up every time. It's a nice dream. I know it's only just a dream but I like to have it. I dreamed it ever since I was a kid."

Dick stopped. He picked up a thin stick and began to scrape dribbles of sand from the castle wall.

"What about Speyer?" Kelly stroked him with her voice. "Remember, you were going to tell us about Speyer."

"It's his fault." A quick anger rose in him. "He got into the dream and it isn't the same anymore. He does it on purpose too. You'd know if you could see him; he's there because he wants to be." Dick kept making little jabs at the castle. The sand was drying out and it crumbled easily. "I never did anything to him. He's got no reason, he's got no reason at all."

"What does he do in the dream?" Kelly touched Dick's arm again.

"Will you believe it if I tell the truth?"

"Yes," Kelly said.

I nodded.

"It started right after he came, a little more all the time till it got the way it is now. I don't know, but I don't think it's going to change anymore. At the start I just had this funny feeling about my mother, but pretty soon I know for sure it isn't her anymore even though I still can't see her. I'm still walking along and it's foggy or smokey now except straight ahead not so much. After a while I see this thing up ahead of me and even though I dream it every time I can never remember what it is until I get up close enough to see. Then I can tell it's a tree that's on fire, except it's only burning on the inside. And I wish I had my shovel even if it wouldn't do any good. I don't want to but I keep on going closer and then all of a sudden there's this thing between me and the tree without any clothes on and it turns around and I see it's him except he's just white skin all over without any way to breathe or talk or see or anything. But it's him all right. He makes me do something bad with him and then he makes me look up in the tree and instead of leaves there's lizards, millions of lizards. They've all got their eyes sewed up shut and they're shivering like the wind was blowing them, but I know the real reason is they're on fire inside just like the tree. And I know I got to warn Mr. Cable and then I know I can't because the last lizard I see looks like me."

We sat there, encircled by the stream noise and our own silence. All that remained of the castle were a few lumpy mounds of sand and a tower. One edge of the turret was seeping away. It wouldn't last too long. Dick spoke again, still remote but hollow now too, as though he had been emptied of something that the rest of his life could not put back into him.

"I think about it in the day sometimes, a lot now really, so days don't help much. I know it's not real or anything but I get scared to go to sleep anymore. It's not right for a person to be scared to go to sleep. Why does he make me dream like that; why does he want to do it?"

"You're right," Kelly said slowly. "It's only a dream. Dreams aren't real. It doesn't mean anything, does it David?"

"No," I said. But I couldn't find the words to joke it away. I wanted to take Kelly's hand and go, but I couldn't make myself touch her. It was her prodding that had severed this from Dick and spliced it to the puzzlement and uneasiness Jimmy had unstrung in me. I couldn't touch her.

"A man shouldn't be able to make you dream like that. He shouldn't be able to. He shouldn't be able to do that." Dick was talking to himself now, running the stick back and forth in front of him. The gouge in the sand was stained dark with moisture at the bottom. Kelly turned away and I followed. Dick was still talking as we left.

We crossed the sand bar and went up the bank, not saying anything. Spurts of dust puffed around our feet as we walked back down the road.

"Why didn't you tell me about Speyer?" Kelly's tone was carefully neutral.

"There wasn't anything to tell."

"And what about now? Isn't there anything to tell now?"

I scuffed at a rock. "No. He's just somebody on the crew. A little older, a little quieter, maybe a little smarter. That's all." I didn't see why I should have to defend or explain anything. And I didn't want to talk about Speyer until I sorted some things out. Or decided there was really nothing to sort.

"But that's not all. You heard Dick, he's terrified of Speyer. And his dream, there has to be something to that. He didn't just make it up out of thin air—he couldn't have. It's really scary, David, the way it fits into my readings. In the tarot, the Fool— "

"Why don't you take those fucking cards and flush them." I was angry, but it came out sharper than I'd meant. "I'm just tired of hearing about them, that's all. If you want to play games, go ahead. But stop pretending it's anything more than that and stop pretending that I'm playing too."

"I'm not playing, David. And we love each other, so whatever it is, you're in it too."

We'd reached the fringe of the meadow. Most of the crew was playing football. The girls they had brought clustered among some trees, just out of range of the end sweeps. Kruger ran one team; some girl was quarterbacking the other. It had Mundeen and seemed to be winning.

"David?"

"I don't want to talk about it."

I was ready to be as hard as I needed to enforce it. But Kelly didn't say anything more. We walked across the meadow, Kelly just perceptibly separating herself from me. When we reached the trees, Karen waved Kelly over and I went on to the keg alone. Stinson was drawing a beer as I came up.

"How's the keg holding out?"

Stinson turned unsteadily, waving a foaming cup.

"Mosely foam. Mike's gonna get another one from somebuzzy's car." He spoke deliberately, but the syllables sloshed into each other.

"You'd better lighten up on that shit." The keg sputtered as I worked it for a beer. "I've got a full load tonight." Scott had thrown up down the side of my car when I hauled him out at the barracks after Kelly's party.

"Me too." He giggled and thumped his stomach. Beer splattered down his shirt. "Shit." He tried to brush off the foam, but most of it had sunk in. "Drunk in the afternoon." He wandered off with an empty cup.

The canyon rock seemed to inhale the sun. Near the keg the dry grass was beaten down, except for a few long tassels gone to seed around one leg of the picnic table. I don't know why I noticed the grass, but I did. And for the first time in my life I believed I would die. Not just knew it as a distant fact, but believed it as a present certainty. Standing there looking down at the grass. Twenty-one years old.

I didn't hear Raylene come up from behind.

The woman's bright blonde hair rose up on her head, lacquered into a dome. She was at least thirty, and very tan.

"I'm Raylene, the sup's sup."

"How do you do"—my eyes flicked over her left hand—"Mrs. Cable. I'm Dave Service."

She sat on the table and handed me an empty cup. "Well, Mr. Service, how about some? Buy me a beer?"

She was wearing shorts, white tennis shoes, and a halter.

"The keg's about shot. Somebody went for another one." Her halter fell away from her skin as she leaned towards me. Her breasts were tanned as far as I could see.

"I'll have some of yours then."

The foam had melted into beer. She took a swallow and eased one leg across the other. She kept looking at me.

"How come a nice kid like you is working for the one-armed

bandit?"

"I'm twenty-one."

"I'm not," she said, and took another swallow. "I won't see twenty anything again, but there are compensations." She shifted on the table, inviting speculation on those compensations. "For one thing, I shoot the damndest game of pool you ever saw. Beat old stumpy so bad he won't even play me." She held the cup out to me; I reached for it but she didn't let go. "Hell of a way to talk about your husband."

"He's your husband," I said carefully.

"That's right, babe, he is that for sure." We both let go at the same time and the cup fell. Raylene started to laugh, hard and high, then cut it off sharply. She pushed herself off the table, picked up the cup, and carefully wiped dirt from the rim on her thigh.

"Maybe you can buy me another one sometime. I like you, lover. You could use a little seasoning, but I like the way you're embarrassed when you look down my front at my tits." She handed me the cup and walked away.

Mundeen came around a bitterbrush thicket, bracing a fresh keg on his shoulder, sweating out the afternoon.

"Give the rabbits any bad ideas?"

I couldn't tell if he meant Kelly or Raylene. "Not that I know of."

"Ummph." He set the keg down on the table and began unscrewing the dead keg's tap. "Bastards won't let me play until I set up the house. Hell of a way to run a party. You run into Cable's old lady yet?"

"Yeah, I guess so."

"Christ, Karen's ready to piss green. Raylene came over first thing and hauled me off to move a couple tables. So we're going along and shit, she's bumping and rubbing like she was in heat. And then she asks if I like what I've been getting off Karen and I say it hasn't worn me down any."

He pulled out the tap and got ready to break into the new keg. It was still early, maybe six o' clock, but the whole canyon was in shadow now except for a wedge of light along the east rim.

"So then I figure, shit, this is my chance to ask something I been wondering about since the first time I saw her and Cable together. I always wanted to know what she thought about that arm of his. You know, what he did with it in bed. And she says hell, he doesn't just keep it on, he uses it. She said it was bigger and stiffer than anything else he had and besides it didn't get the sheets wet. Flattened my dick like a pancake."

He punched the keg and it hissed alive.

"Got any idea how they get along?"

"Who, Cable and Miss Bump and Rub?"

"Yeah."

"Nobody's ever been dumb enough to try to move in and find out. For sure this horse knows better."

"Doesn't Cominsky know them pretty well?"

"Cominsky wouldn't say shit if his mouth was full of it." Mike handed me a cup of beer. "How come you're asking?"

"No special reason."

"Shit, she'd grind you up so fine Cable wouldn't have to bother." Mike finished his beer and drew another. Shouts rang off the canyon walls as Moya ducked and scrambled away from Kruger for a touchdown. The game was breaking up. Mike sucked a great mouthful of beer.

"Listen, my first year this dude from the crew took her up on the come-on. Big stud, too. The police picked him up one morning trying to get to the hospital. Stark fucking naked and stone sober. His cock was swoll up like a loaf of bread. She bit the bastard. Just laid her teeth right on the money and bit him." Mike shook his head, impressed.

"Never did come back to camp for his stuff. No, you just stick with Kelly. She's a little weird maybe, but it don't look like she bites."

"No," I said. "Not so far."

Mike punched me on the shoulder and we walked back to the others.

The party had throttled back, waiting for the hanging heat to thin in the evening wind. The oak and pockets of scrub pine, embalmed in dust, twitched in the first breeze. Mike said he could get a ride with someone else; Kelly was talking to Karen and wanted to stay. I watched a hawk tilt into the wind and ride it up in a circling climb. He worked upcanyon, finally vanishing over the horizon of the rim. I finished my beer and started for Dalton. As I pulled onto the road, I looked in my rearview mirror. Pitkin was coming slowly toward the meadow, a shadow in the decaying light.

———

VI

It was dark by the time I reached the highway and turned toward Dalton. Carved out of cliffsides, the road was a killer: no shoulders, random guard rails, tight curves, rockfalls. Driving it in daylight, you could pick up the occasional glints, far down, of wrecks that were never hauled up.

As I swung into the Santa Sangres, I thought of Pitkin's blank silhouette in the mirror and of his dream. And what it had to do with anything that was true. I hadn't had much real contact with Speyer, but even before this he seemed to exert almost a gravitational attraction. There was a consistent texture to him, as though for him intention and act were woven into one piece. It was hard to factor him into any sort of relationship with Pitkin. Still, one-sided or reciprocal, the involvement existed for Dick.

The possible readings of Dick's dream tangled themselves in blurry speculation. Was Speyer the haunting father that Dick hadn't spoken of? Did Dick see him as some threat to his waking dream, a permanent position with the Forest Service? Was it all psychological fabrication— old emotional debris engorged by the distortions of Dick's mind? And a last option, intricate, on the fringe of chance. Was it possible that something substantial connected Pitkin and Speyer—perhaps Jimmy and maybe Kelly too? Something at the murky edge of believability?

The owl hit the windshield before I could even back off the gas.

A shape in the headlights, the thump, then a smear on the glass, a few small feathers stuck to it. I stopped, shaken. I lit a cigarette, then got out and walked back. The owl was in the road. Even under the flashlight it looked like a perfect replica of the live bird, the only sign of violence a thread of blood from its beak. Taking the owl by the legs, I slung it over the side.

As I walked back to the car, I turned the flashlight on my palm. I had felt a sting as I let the owl go. My hand, scored diagonally across the palm from the talons, was bleeding freely. I blotted it on my jeans, wondering if I should worry about rabies.

The rocks had come down a few hundred feet up the road, just past the apex of a curve. Not up to speed yet, I veered around the first few and stopped easily before reaching the main slide. Rolling, lifting, levering, I had a path cleared by the time another car came. Three of us muscled the bigger rocks back against the cliff or over the edge, opening both lanes. I drove the rest of the way cautious and edgy, both hands on the wheel.

It was late when I finally pulled in to Dalton. The bunkhouse was dark, and I banged a shin before finding the light switch. The room was empty. Most of the crew would stay in town after the party broke up. As I was pulling the sheets off my bunk, a bank of lights went out and I walked across to the utility shed to change the fuse.

The shed was a cramped museum of cobwebs, spare parts, and derelict equipment—everything but an extra fuse. While I was rummaging, I noticed a piece of cloth wedged in an unfinished space behind a ceiling joist. It seemed a likely enough place for fuses, and I tugged the bag out. In it was a box of ammunition, two clips, and a Luger. The pistol had a film of oil on it and the barrel felt like a snake. It was loaded. I slid it back into the bag, at the last moment wiping my fingerprints from the butt, and stuffed the bag up where I had found it.

I walked back to the barracks, not wanting to try to straighten out one more thing, remembering Cable saying at fire school that anyone who thought this was going to be like a summer at camp had better take his teddy bear and go home. The warning was beginning to take on dimension.

Jimmy was sitting on his bunk when I came in. I was surprised to find him there. In the last weeks, he'd spent less and less time in the barracks. Often, he was not there at lights-out and gone before the rest of us were up. I wondered if he knew about the pistol, or about me finding it. I started to talk about the party, and although he watched me closely, he wasn't listening. My account dwindled to an awkward silence. My palm still stung from the talon slice. Handling a shovel was going to hurt. I finished making up my bunk, asked if Jimmy minded, and turned off the lights.

"I remember my grandfather speaking." In the dark, Jimmy's voice seemed directionless, as though it didn't come from a single source in the room. It brought me out of a haze of half sleep.

"About how brave it takes to be a man. Not brave to kill. That is little. But by yourself brave in the heart. How life can take all you have gathered from you but never what you are. The way understanding the truth of what gambles with us is how brave in yourself must happen. How the lie is everywhere in front and sucks at us because it is large and easy and we want to give ourselves away. To come to the edge of the village of truth— this is where the lie is the most beautiful city, but if a man passes into the village and looks back he sees the lie is only what it is, ugly and useless like the baby hole of an old woman. How my grandfather speaking to me when I was a child, dark and full of others."

His voice, bracketed by silence, seemed to create a volatile pressure in the room that a wrong word or even a gesture in the dark might detonate.

"I don't understand," I said finally. "I mean, I believe you, I just don't know what it has to do with me."

I waited for a response, then tried again. "I'm not even sure what we're talking about. I guess some things could seem a little strange if you looked at them that way. I don't know."

I tried to sort out what I wanted to say, but couldn't. I'd just have to listen to it come out and try to adjust as I went along. Jimmy sounded absolutely sincere, but the chance that he was playing some obscure game with me or was neurotically disfigured skittered around as possibilities. He said little around the crew, but his language was mostly straightforward. The idiom of these monologues seemed to take on the contours of a jerky translation from another language. Compounding that, his content was elliptical, rarely offering hard, verifiable footholds. I went back to the night in the truck and one solid piece of ground. If I could get that straight, maybe the rest of it would come clear.

"What really happened to Cable's arm?"

Jimmy let out a long breath. Then, with a spiny voice: "Maybe I make a mistake of you. Maybe I make a mistake now. I will tell you these things. Cable's arm burned off him in the medicine house where he went to be healed when he was shot in that place Korea. My brother Amos died time ago fifteen years in that fire men call Tentongue Canyon. What is true now are boys. Some brave to kill even. Boys where what must be done is more maybe than men can do even. You must throw down your mind. A hawk does not study the wind; the earth dreams itself awake in the first season. How seeds find the earthbed without teaching, and water knows its way by heart. I tell to you these things and one more. I can not speak what you must know before it is you know it. Then I never will have to."

This time Jimmy stopped with finality. Nothing more would be said. I lay awake a long time. A light wind drew small sounds from the bunkhouse. Between its eddies, I listened to the strong, even breathing of Jimmy, asleep. He was right. Whatever I needed to know now was nothing he could tell me.

In the morning I was sick. Fever, a bitter taste in my mouth, an unruly gut. I tried to drink some juice as the last of the crew straggled in. Even Cable was late. When he arrived, Cable told us to run the course without timing ourselves, just to finish it. He told Perez, Snead, and Calendar to stick around.

I threw up outside the mess hall. Too weak and dizzy to even walk the course, I went back to the barracks. I slid in and out of sleep most of the morning, carrying dreams from one fragment of sleep to the next. By afternoon I was shaky, but better. I went up to the mess hall, thinking I should eat something if I could. Bailey was sweeping up, jabbing the broom around erratically.

"Service, say, everybody is working up at Crystal Lake. Cable said I should find you something to do if you ever stopped puking. Say, you look bad. Maybe you should have some coffee.

I managed to keep down a piece of toast and some water. Bailey circled the room, swiping the broom under the tables.

"Say, that must have been some party. Like my daddy used to say, if you can't hold it, fold it. You heard what happened with Snead and Perez? No, I guess you didn't. Calendar too."

His talk ravelled out and there was a sluggish gap for me between hearing and understanding, the words taking the long way around in my head.

"Say, did Cable stick it to them. Let them know they better think twice about dogging it again like they did in that playoff or whatever you guys did with China Hat. Said if they screwed around anymore he'd ship them down the hill. Snead lipped off and was going to take him on. Something about Cable not being his jailer. Calendar got him out of there. Good thing too. Say, I seen what Cable can do. That's what comes of having a criminal on the crew. I told Cable that."

I still felt too queasy to do anything in Bailey's kitchen. I was going to lie down again, but the bunkhouse was hot and stale. I went out and turned up the ridge, moving slowly up the slope away from the obstacle course until I came on a compact stand of oak and some fugitive pine from the high country. The grove nested in a small notch in the ridge and a thin wind came through it. The place eased the foreground out of my thoughts. Behind it was an image of Raylene, bending toward me at the party. I took the image to sleep with me.

I woke up with only a chip of the dream left. In it, I was hidden, watching some woman I didn't know take off her clothes. I felt aroused and guilty, then became aware that I was there to protect her from someone else who was also watching.

Walking back, I still had a little rubbery give in my knees but I felt better, and hungry. The crew pulled into the compound as I came down. I took some shots about my hangover and let it go that way. It was easier than trying to explain whatever it was— some odd bug, something I'd eaten at the party. I'd had enough hangovers to know that this was something else. I'd meant to ask Jimmy if owl talons carried infections; now, I didn't want to risk another installment of his augury, and besides the cut hardly hurt, just a ribbon of scab outlined faintly in red.

After supper, most of the crew settled into a mild, post-party slump. I talked with Jarvis for a while about the forestry program at Humboldt State. I would graduate next year, and I had already pretty well decided that I didn't want to go on in English. The prospect of spending five years writing a dissertation on comma faults in the Eighteenth Century heroic couplet while coercing grudging freshmen to write complete sentences seemed less an unappealing apprenticeship than a dismal prelude to a career much like it. With most of my general requirements out of the way, it looked like I could get a B.S. in forestry in two years. Jarvis was specializing in timber management and was at Dalton because of some computer foulup in the Regional Office on his summer employment application. He had put in for work in timber management on the Shasta-Trinity. Pete didn't plan to work for the Forest Service after he finished school. The money was a lot better in industry, he said, and you didn't have those ecology freaks messing around with your management programs.

The talk with Jarvis helped me put the summer into perspective. Whatever quirky channels it took were diversions in my life, not the mainstream. After September, whatever happened here would belong to itself again. I could choose to replay it in memory or let it pass out of my life altogether. I could almost talk myself into seeing the summer so plainly. Only Jimmy thickened against that interpretation, resisting reduction to something incidental.

Later in the evening, Stinson came down from the mess hall and said Cable wanted to see me. I wondered if he believed that I'd really been sick, not just hungover like everyone else.

His office was in a small room tacked onto the mess hall. I hadn't been in it before. He was looking at some papers when I knocked and went in. A bunk from the barracks was wedged into a corner, and it struck me that he'd been spending more nights there the last few weeks.

"I didn't get a chance at the party," he pushed the papers back on his desk, "but I wanted to let you know you did a damn good job the other day. Matter of fact, I like what I've seen on the line. You never can tell who's going to amount to something, and you have."

Already, he'd said nearly as much to me as he had so far all season. And although what he said might have been true, it was not what he wanted me here for. He was too direct not to seem evasive when he was being that way. At least it wasn't going to be about the phantom hangover. He wouldn't circle around any taint of sloughing off.

"You know, this could turn out to be the best crew I've had at Dalton." He stopped again.

"I noticed on your application here you're going to college to be a teacher. How come you hired on with Uncle?"

Cable was off-balance enough that I felt safe in holding back, not telling him more than I had to until I found out what he wanted.

"I needed to make some money. I thought I'd see what this kind of work was like."

"Yeah, well it's shitty work and you could make more money picking up pop bottles along the highway. Shit." Cable banged his arm down on the desk. He pulled out a bottle of bourbon from a drawer and poured some into two coffee cups.

"Here."

I took the cup, but didn't drink.

"If I was any good talking out both sides of my mouth, I'd be grabbing secretaries' butts in the Regional Office by now."

He drained off the cup and I took a hard swallow in self-defense. I felt as vulnerable as I had the first day of fire school when he'd kicked my feet out from under me for bowing my back doing push-ups.

"OK. This is what it comes to. It could be that Snead's got a pistol up here. If it turns up, he's out of business and he knows it. That sort of thing doesn't go over real big with parole officers or with me either. He's a tough kid and he makes a damn good firefighter. You out-tough him and treat him fair and he'll do a job. So what I want you to do is keep your eyes open. He told me he didn't have one stashed, and I don't think he's lying. But he might be. And if he is, I want to know about it."

A bolt of adrenalin pumped through me at the word "pistol." If Cable had stopped there, I would have told him about it. I'm not sure why I didn't anyway.

"Why. . . ."

"You?" Cable was looking at me straight on. "Because I think I can count on you. And because I'm telling you to."

He waited for me to say something. I nodded, which seemed to be enough.

"Well, see you in the morning." He raked the papers back in front of him and I got up.

"The old lady thinks you're a good-looking kid."

I turned back, wondering what was showing on my face.

"Not that I can say much for her taste in men, so don't let it go to your head." He grinned, holding it just a fraction longer than was comfortable.

I walked for a while before going back to the bunkhouse. Stinson asked what Cable had wanted. I told him he wanted to know whether Stinson was still beating off in the john. Scott made the mistake of denying it. Moya and Mundeen jumped in, and Stinson finally beat a retreat to the mess hall under a barrage of laughter.

I'd slept enough during the day that sleep came hard that night. I tried to rerun the summer, but incidents called up others, connective sequences blurred, and answers were indistinguishable from hunches. The talk with Jarvis, the sense of a solid future built of consecutive steps toward a goal, so tangible only hours ago felt remote now. Ambiguities and my place in them, the whole tangling present, asserted itself like an imperative.

What was clear were the hard questions. Did Jimmy in fact have access to some different, more accurate region of understanding? Or was he a misplaced relic, maybe fraudulent, fringing between a half-invented past and bleary old age? Was Pitkin vulnerable to dreams because he was defective, naive, or did his simpleness open him up to possibilities beyond the range of the commonplace? What did Speyer have to do with any of this? Or Kelly? Was it all an either/or construction, or would the truth be visible only in shadings? And perhaps the most important question of all. How vitally did all of this, any of them, concern me, and what was I going to do about it? I slept, finally, the blankets knotted around me.

In the morning, still more asleep than awake, it came to me that much in these puzzlements converged on Speyer. If I could satisfy myself about him, the rest might fall into place.

When I went in for breakfast, Speyer was eating with Perez and Calendar. I sat with Jarvis, Cavenaugh, and Cominsky. Cavenaugh was talking about the fir, cedar, and hemlock forests of the Northwest. How every draw had a running stream— not the dry, rockstrewn rubble of flash floods that passed for creeks in the Santa Sangres. A lush land that gave more than it took. Jarvis asked why he left. Cavenaugh shrugged.

"You stay someplace till it itches. You wake up one morning with the same hangover from drinking in the same bar with the same people telling the same stories you heard last week. Likely there hasn't been a new woman in town for months, not counting hippies. Pretty soon you're itching in ways the place can't scratch. That's when it's time to move on."

After our morning workout, we rode up to Crystal Lake for more project work. While most of the crew dug a new water line, three of us bucked up firewood for the campsites. Cavenaugh ran the chain saw while Snead and I quartered the rounds with axes and pitched them in the back of a pickup. Cavenaugh ran the big McCulloch with the efficient nonchalance of a pro. He said if you worked in the woods you got as used to running a saw as city people did a power mower. He let me try it for a while. On my first cut, I pinched the bar when the log came together on it. After Cavenaugh pounded the cut open with a wedge, I gouged the chain into some rocks finishing the cut through the bottom of the log. That shut us down for a while until Cavenaugh had refiled the teeth.

Just before lunch, he dropped a dying Ponderosa pine, three feet through at the butt. The tree was leaning toward some picnic tables and a fenced walk. With side cuts and wedges, Cavenaugh coaxed it away from its natural line of fall, bringing it around so it swivelled on its base coming down, dropping near our pile of rounds. Cavenaugh grinned.

"Wasn't sure I could do it. It's been a while, and these dead whores got rot in them sometimes that makes them screwy to figure."

He started to unlace his protective chaps. "But I guess once you got the feel for it, it's like pushing the right buttons on a woman. Women and timber, don't matter how big or how fancy—you tickle them in the right spots and they all lay down for you right where you want them."

Snead hadn't talked much all morning. As we ate lunch, I said something about Cable. Snead sailed the rest of his sandwich toward the pine stump.

"That crippled prick's got it in for me." He took a bite of an apple, then sidearmed it at the stump too.

"Bailey must get these soggy fuckers at the dump."

I asked him about Cable.

"He can hardly wait to ship me back to the joint. Somebody told him I was carrying a piece."

"Are you?" I said it before I could wonder whether I should.

"Shit. Sure I do. I keep one around in case I ever want to knock off the pop machine." He coughed and spit. "I never carried iron. Even when I was dumb enough to get busted, I was smart enough not to do that. The laws they got now, you get caught on a job with a piece, you got yourself enough time to choke on it. It's like Calendar says, they get you down once, they ain't never gonna let you back up. The bastard knows he's got me by the short hairs. If I split, they lock me up. Even this chain gang's got the slammer beat a mile."

From what Cable had said, I didn't think he held anything against Snead, but I couldn't think of any convincing way to tell Snead that. Everybody knew he'd been in prison, but no one seemed to know what he'd done. Cominsky heard that he'd knifed someone after they'd stolen a car together. Someone else thought he'd robbed a liquor store. Whatever it was, Snead wore his history in a set of reptilian eyes: a fierce surface laid down over something sub-zero. I tried to sound offhand.

"What'd they arrest you for?"

Snead looked at me hard, then laughed. "Man, you wouldn't last twenty-four hours on the street. I'll tell you this; it wasn't for boosting hubcaps."

As we came down in the truck from Crystal Lake, we could see the gray-brown chamber of smog, blanking out everything in the basin below three thousand feet. It followed the canyon contours almost that high into the Santa Sangres, the death line for pines moving up a little every year. Dalton lay just above its maximum reach. Fighting fire in the lower country, on bad days, the air felt like acid in your lungs.

The excitement of beating China Hat faded quickly. We hadn't been on the line for a while, and by the end of the week we were restless and stale. The days were clogged with heat and a clutter of meaningless projects. The obstacle course was now more drudgery than challenge. No one pushed to better his time on it. There was more sourness about things we ignored or passed off earlier in the summer, and talk often turned toward what people would do when the season was over.

Some of us had our mail picked up once a week at the ranger station in Glendora. The checks that came in now were the first without any fire time on them. Most of us were GS-3's and made $2.85 an hour. Even though the checks covered two weeks, without overtime they didn't amount to much. Moya came into the bunkhouse one night, his check folded into an airplane. He sailed it in a wobbling arc down the room.

"It's a bird, it's a plane, it's the Mex' super check."

The plane veered into a locker and Moya retrieved it.

"This is so much money I wish I had more." Moya recreased the paper and sailed it to Stinson. It passed around the barracks before colliding with Perez, coming in from outside.

"What's this shit?"

"Oh, you're so bad," said Moya, dancing up and lifting the check from Perez' hand. "I'm gonna buy myself a new Chevy with this and take away Rosa from you. But you're so ugly, maybe I'll only have to buy a Volkswagen."

"Fuck you, Mouse," said Perez, grinning.

"Oh, but you talk so slick I don't know if Rosa would listen to my line."

"Shit," said Perez, taking a good-natured swipe at Moya.

"Say your prayers, Sunshine." Moya went into a crouch, fists up, and weaved in front of Perez. "Except you're so ugly I'll be ashamed to make you look any worse."

Perez turned half away, then lunged back grabbing Moya. He slung him over his shoulder, grabbed his ankles, then swung him in a circle three or four times. He finished holding Moya suspended in front of him.

"Your mouth is gonna get you killed one of these days." He tapped Moya's head on the floor. "Just like Danny Estrada, except worse." He tapped his head once more, harder. "You ready to quit now?"

"Sure," said Moya. He reached up between Perez' legs and grabbed. Perez howled, let go of Moya, and folded up.

"You little fucker, you busted them." He went down to his knees, holding his crotch, rocking.

"No way," said Moya, scrambling out of reach. "Everybody knows Rosa already done that."

Perez looked up at him, murderous.

"I take that back," said Moya quickly. He went over to his duffle bag and pulled out a pint of tequila. "Here." He handed the bottle to Perez who took a long drink.

"Except you're my partner, someday I'm gonna have to bust you up."

"I know," said Moya.

Calendar had ended up holding Moya's check. He unfolded it and read off the numbers.

"One hundred ninety-six dollars and forty-seven cents." He tossed the check on Moya's bunk. "Just enough to keep you off the streets and part of somebody's profit margin. A little more grease for the machine."

Moya jammed the check in his duffle bag without saying anything.

"The government's got one sweet deal for itself." Calendar lit a cigarette. He had chain smoked since fire school, and coughed raggedly before he spoke.

"You bet they do. Slave wages for the kind of work most men wouldn't do for ten dollars an hour. Straight pay for overtime, no hazard pay, no insurance, and fifty cents an hour for keeping us locked up on standby, standby pay for standby fires. Prime beef, two cents a pound on the hoof. And they know how to keep us coming back, how to keep sucking us in. Dangle the rainbow of a permanent appointment, make this sound like a glory job, like we're some kind of heroes; a guaranteed job every season as long as your body holds out, enough unemployment checks to buy beer and beans in the winter."

Calendar had started in flat, unemotional tones. As he got into it, his voice was flecked with bitterness.

"They pass out red cards in June, take them back in September. And look what they get. Not just here but all over the West. A supply of migrant labor they can count on every season to save billions of dollars worth of lumber for the timber companies. Keep the woods green so the bourgeois can spend a few more billion to pretend they're having fun, to keep from thinking about their lives. Bleed a few more dollars out of us in taxes to pay for slaughtering women and children in Asia or anywhere else people make the mistake of being the wrong color to want freedom. And keep us in prime shape so they can collect our bodies and send them around the world to kill and be killed with bullets we bought for ourselves. A sweet deal with a crooked deck. Eat shit and pretend it's gravy. Translate the Latin on the dollar bill and you get the motto of capitalism."

"So deal yourself out." Mundeen was stretched across his bunk, working out with dumbbells. "Anybody who doesn't like it here knows where the road starts."

"Sure," said Calendar, coughing. "Perez and Moya can go back to the barrio. Lots of chances there. Nelly can go suck his Dad's dick and never grow up. Pitkin can find out what the real world does with people with 80 IQ's. Snead can go back to jail. And the gentry can go back to college after slumming it a while, play pattycake with their student deferments, and learn how to keep the system running."

"Look," said Mundeen, sitting up. "Nothing's perfect. Nobody owes you anything. You make your own way or you don't. Whining about money and the government's not going to change a thing. Working on this crew doesn't have anything to do with money. It's got to do with pride and getting the job done, whatever it takes. That's something you can't buy or sell or ever take away from somebody. Shit." Mundeen belched, embarrassed. "I sound like some kind of asshole preacher." He belched again and looked at Calendar. "But that beats sounding like a plain asshole."

Calendar lit another cigarette and shook his head. "They've got us right where they want us—under their heel and licking it. Someday you're going to wake up and look in the mirror and wonder where the bootprint came from."

"Someday you're gonna find yourself kicked halfway to L.A. and you're not going to have to wonder where the bootprint on your butt came from."

"Yeah," said Kruger, "if you don't like it here, go to Russia. You can fight fire for the Commies for ten cents an hour and get sent to Siberia if you don't like it."

Calendar shrugged. "You believe the lie long enough...." He stopped and shrugged again; got up and walked out of the bunkhouse.

"Who put a quarter in him?" asked Stinson.

"He plays his own tune," said Kruger, rooting at an itch in his armpit. "And one of these days, somebody's gonna pull his plug."

"What do you think about that shit?" Mundeen aimed the question at me. "All that stuff about the system ripping us off. I took a course in American history and they don't teach it anything like that."

"The only way you passed history," said Kruger, "is because O'Brien likes jocks and you bought a term paper."

"Piss off," said Mundeen. "If things are like Calendar says, a professor would know about it; they get paid to know that kind of stuff. Calendar's just like fans who can't stand it if you don't win every game. You win ten games running the veer, they think you should run the wishbone the first time you lose one. We get a few of them like Calendar at San Jose; we just ship them on up to Berkeley where they can run around screaming about things and it doesn't matter because everybody's like that up there." Mundeen hitched himself around on his bunk. "You go to one of those poison ivy schools; you must have got a ration of that shit. It doesn't really stack up to anything, does it?"

"I don't know," I said. "I guess it's something to think about."

"You can think till your brains fall out," said Kruger. "Then you can talk just like Calendar."

I let it alone and nothing more was said.

Through the week, I had been trying to work out an approach to Speyer. The questions I wanted to ask were too odd or unformulated to deal with directly. An oblique approach required a certain companionship, and it was turning out to be hard to see how I was going to manage that. Speyer wasn't available for that kind of contact. He was seldom in the bunkhouse; when he was, he read or slept, removed from the locker room jousting. He ate with Calendar and Perez, and often walked alone up the ridge after supper or spent time in Cable's office. On project work he was congenial but remote, seeming to be wholly aware but only partly present. Sometimes, he appeared amused. I had talked to him now and then, and although he was always attentive, it felt as though he was withdrawing his attention from something else to focus it on me.

One night, at the beginning of our fourth week without a fire, Mundeen collected some of the crew for an expedition. He wouldn't tell anyone what he was up to except to say that he had signed on to fight fire, not mow lawns at the ranger station, and he was going to do something about it.

Those of us who didn't go were draped around the bunkhouse, the room stagnant with heat. Stinson had been trying to master a card trick he had learned from a book he ordered. It required dexterity and memory, and he was having a hard time getting it down. So far, only Pitkin had been fooled. He was wrestling with the deck when Speyer asked if he could try his hand at it. Speyer did three tricks, each more baffling than the last. He showed Stinson how he did one of them. Stonecrofter asked if he would do some more.

"Hey," said Stinson, "Do one where you make money appear."

"Do one where you make Kruger disappear," said Moya. "Except make it so he never comes back."

"Kruger's out with his boyfriend," said Stinson. "Why don't you make Service vanish. He's such a lightweight you shouldn't have any trouble."

I noticed Pitkin at the far end of the bunkhouse, watching, pretending to concentrate on something he was whittling.

"I don't think I could manage that," said Speyer. He sounded a trace uneasy now at the attention centered on him.

"Well do something," said Stonecrofter.

"Yeah, do one more so we don't have to watch Stinson wreck another deck."

"Something different." Stonecrofter was excited.

"OK, one more," said Speyer, looking around. "I'll need a wooden match."

Moya plundered his pack until he found a box. Speyer took out a match and rolled it between his thumb and fingers. He reached up suddenly and struck it on the stiff side of his face. Then holding the match in front of him, he somehow bent the flame until it was almost horizontal and made it follow his finger around in a circle, the upper yellow of the flame deepening toward red as it moved. He snapped his fingers and the match went out.

"Jesus," said Stonecrofter, "how'd you do that? That was really something."

"It's magic, man." Moya's eyes widened in appreciation. "That wasn't some card trick shuck, that was magic."

Some whoops carried up from the direction of the ravine where Mundeen had gone.

"There's not much to it," said Speyer, picking up a book from his bunk. "A little sleight of hand, a little illusion."

Mundeen entered triumphantly, hands cupped around something, the others trailing after him. He walked over to Stonecrofter's bunk and opened his hands. The horned toad leaped past Stonecrofter's head, landing on his pillow. Nelson squealed and jumped away. Mundeen scooped up the toad before it could launch itself again.

"No more pulling weeds," said Mundeen, heading for the door. "No more painting shitters or piling brush. This," he said turning, "is gonna get us back where we belong, back on the line." We followed him outside, down near the tool shed where Kruger waited with a can of saw gas. Cominsky was walking a little ahead of me.

"What's the deal?" I asked him.

"They're gonna burn it."

"Why? Burn it how?"

The door to the mess hall banged and Cable came down the steps with Bailey.

"It's like a tradition or something," Cominsky said. "Every season since I been here, when there aren't any fires sooner or later somebody rounds up a toad and torches it off. Often as not, we end up rolling the next day or two. This ain't so bad. One season they couldn't find any toads. So some of the guys decided this one joker nobody liked looked a lot like a toad. We had latrines back then, and they hauled him out back and hung him down the shitter by his ankles. They couldn't figure out how to do anything like burning him without really hurting him. He quit after that anyway, and we got some fires."

"Ok, circle up," said Mundeen, standing with Kruger. "No, you shitheads, all the way around." We shuffled into a lopsided ring around them. Cable and Bailey came up, joining the circle.

"Everybody here?" Cable asked.

"Count off," said Mundeen.

Jimmy, Speyer, and Pitkin were missing.

"Somebody go up to the bunkhouse and get them."

"Jimmy's off somewhere in the brush," said Stinson. "I saw him go after supper."

"Go up and get the rest of them."

Stinson sprinted up to the bunkhouse and came back followed by Pitkin. "Speyer's not there."

"Ok," said Cable. "Go ahead on it."

Mundeen spread his legs a little and raised his cupped hands above his head. "The Great Toad is fat and pisshappy. He squats in the woods and pisses on everything and because of him nothing will burn. So we're gonna have a toad toast and pucker his pecker so he can't use it for a while; cook his cock so we can get back in business." Years in the locker room gave his phrasing a sort of profane eloquence. Mundeen brought his hands down.

"Everybody sit down; tighten it up so there aren't any spaces. He's got to stay in the circle. If you let him out, Nelly, you're gonna wish your mother had an abortion instead of you."

There was some loud laughter with a strain of nervousness in it. Mundeen reached down, sloshing the toad with saw gas. Kruger struck a match and dropped it on the toad as Mundeen released it. The toad lunged into the air, flaming.

"Burn, fucker, burn!" screamed Mundeen. Kruger, then some of the rest picked up the chant. The toad plunged across the dirt, headed toward Moya and Perez. A wild, veering leap took it in front of Snead. He lifted his leg and brought his boot heal down, but the toad had lurched away.

"Burn! Burn, you bastard!" It rose straight up then, maybe three feet, in a last withering leap. In the dirt, it jerked a little, but soon the only motion was the light skimming its skin as the saw gas burned out.

"All right," said Mundeen. "All mothering right. Now we're gonna get some action."

It was as though we were welded in the circle until the last blue gust of flame was gone. Pitkin broke away first and the rest of us followed. As we walked back to the barracks, Jarvis said to no one, everyone:

"Senseless. Senseless and sick. Jesus Christ, I can't believe it."

"A frog can't feel nothing," said Stinson.

"Senseless."

An unlikely commentator, Cavenaugh spoke into the hollow of the word. "Things happen whether they make sense or not. They just happen, that's all. You go around looking for reasons, you got a long way to go."

Moya danced up the steps to the bunkhouse, grabbed the doorjam and swung in. "Dee dah. Now we're gonna cook. I think I better read a book so I can remember how to use a shovel."

When I came in, Pitkin was lying on his bunk, faced away from the room. I walked down the aisle and sat on the next bunk.

"Dick? You OK?"

He kept facing the wall.

"You feel all right?"

"I didn't have to do it." His voice was pinched and toneless. "Nobody could make me. I didn't have to."

"That's right," I said, getting up. I didn't want to draw attention to Dick. I couldn't think of what to say or ask anyway. "It was just a game. . . like the other seasons. . . ." His shoulders were hunched as though he were trying to shield himself from a blow. I walked away.

I went up to the mess hall and poured out some coffee. Adding water and sugar to the silt made it drinkable. Speyer came in as I was finishing the cup.

"You missed the burning."

"So I hear," said Speyer. "Is there any more coffee?"

"If you can stand it."

He poured a cup and stirred in some sugar.

"What did you think of it?" He sat down across the table from me.

"The burning? I don't know. A little gruesome, pretty harmless."

"The toad might think otherwise." Speyer said it without accusation, as though it were something I might have said myself. "You're right, though," he went on, "there's really not much harm in it. It's a little like praying or sex or voting, say—a gesture implying control, connection with something that's really out of our hands."

There was something synthetic about Speyer's speaking, as though English wasn't his native tongue but a language he'd mastered and now knew almost too well. What was missing were the quirks that give our voices inflection.

"It might even have been worthwhile. Living on top of each other like this builds up a ghetto effect after a while. The pressure needs to be drained off. A fire, a party, a toad-burning—they all let the belt out a notch or two. I imagine that's why Cable encourages the ceremony." He took a sip of coffee.

"If they'd really wanted to be malicious, they'd have dropped the toad in Bailey's coffee." He took another sip, squinting at the taste.

"I thought that's what Bailey made his coffee out of anyway."

Speyer smiled and shook his head. "How Bailey gets coffee to taste like this defies imagination. And you should never ask what you'd rather not know."

I nodded. "Speaking of knowing, you did some pretty fancy burning yourself tonight. How much of a trick is there to that?"

Speyer moved his hand in modest disparagement. "Just a little discrete exhaling through your nose. I'll show you sometime if you like."

"What about the way you changed the color of the flame?"

"Ah, that," said Speyer. "Most people don't notice. But I'm afraid that's proprietary information. It took me a long time to refine that little turn."

We walked back to the barracks together.

"Cominsky was saying they'd burned toads before, and that sometimes there were fires afterwards."

"Never discount the power of coincidence," said Speyer. "Or the predictive value of statistics. Cable knows the dates of every fire on the Forest for the last ten years. It wouldn't surprise me if that had something to do with the timing of this."

Two days later, we rolled on the Skyhook Fire. It was called in by a fire prevention guard, finishing his patrol for the day. The fire had started from a pile of cigarette butts dumped off the shoulder of Skyhook Road. The prevention guard had knocked it down with the slip-on pumper unit in his pickup, but ran out of water before he could control it. We reached the fire at dusk. It was moving spottily up a steep slope, flaring where it reached concentrations of manzanita.

"Easy money," said Moya. "Another picnic in the woods."

Cable divided the crew and we began working up, lining both flanks, pinching towards the head of the fire. Within a couple of hours, we had narrowed the fire front to a few hundred feet. There was little heat or smoke, and yucca bases provided a show as we grubbed a line up the rocky slope. Every so often, one would burn through and cartwheel down on its spiny leaves, streaming sparks like a runaway fireworks display. The road was broad enough to catch them, so we didn't have to worry about fire carrying below us. Rocks, too, were beginning to come down through the burn as roots charred away. By now, we were above most of them and outside their main line of fall.

We had less than a hundred feet of line to finish when the fire head scuttled through a patch of bitterbrush and made a run up a small dead-end draw. My half of the crew was suddenly beneath the fire. The scrapers began carving a trench, knowing we couldn't make it wide enough to stop a yucca that had gotten up any speed. We'd have to trace the path of any that got by, mopping up the embers before they caught in the unburned fuel beneath us.

Cable scouted ahead. When he came back, he said the fire was cut off in the draw which ended in vertical rock walls on three sides. We'd have it contained as soon as we tied off the line to the cliffs on either side of the mouth of the ravine.

The first yucca came down just after Cable got back. It gained speed until it was bounding extravagantly, as much as ten feet down the slope with each arc.

"I got it," shouted Moya, moving over to where the yucca would intersect the line. "It's mine."

At the last moment, the yucca deflected off a rock and pinwheeled at a new angle. Moya launched himself out of his crouch, shovel extended full length. He stopped the yucca above the line and cradled it in the shovel as he fell.

"Hey," said Moya, scrambling up, "with a shortstop like me we're gonna win the pennant. Mr. Cable, I think maybe I should see if my agent can get me a better deal next year."

"Nice stop," said Cable.

"All glove, no bat," said Perez. "He can't hit his mouth with a fork."

"All mouth," said Kruger.

"All world," said Moya, trying to get his headlamp to work again.

Cable put us back to work. We'd nearly tied the line off when the rockfall cut loose. It started near the head of the ravine and accelerated down the chute-like corridor. Falling rock was what we feared most on the line. In timbered country, you could find a tree shield. In the open brush, you could only wait and dodge. In the dark, wait and dodge was a lethal game. We could hear the thunk and rumble as the rocks plunged down, glazing more rocks into motion as they came, but you could predict little from the sound.

We tensed, our headlamps shifting across the scant brush above us. It was over in maybe not more than a minute. The largest rock I saw was the size of a stove. The big ones were easy. With their weight and momentum, they established a line you could count on and avoid. The smaller ones, say the size of your head, were the killers. They hurtled erratically out of the darkness, glancing berserkly. At thirty miles an hour, these rocks didn't just break whatever they hit—they maimed it. I had seen a convict coming off the line earlier in the season. He had been hit in the forearm. The arm had been uprooted from the shoulder socket, and the bones above his wrist jutted out through pulpy flesh.

Any of us could have been hit. None of us was. We listened as the rocks finished their run to the road.

"I thought we was playing for fun," said Moya. "Them guys," he said soberly, "was playing for keeps."

Cable pulled us back from the line as soon as we tied it off. We watched the fire through the night, but didn't go back into the burn to mop up as more rocks harvested the hillside.

When we got back to Dalton in the morning, some mail had come in. Moya opened his and swore quietly in Spanish. Perez and Stinson had similar letters. All of them had been drafted.

———

VII

The Skyhook Fire had carried into our weekend. The fire weather forecast predicted a weak Pacific front the following day, bringing humidities up, dropping temperatures into the 70's. We poked around most of the day putting our fire tools and gear back in shape, waiting to see whether we'd be released from standby and could start for town at 4:30.

The draft notices laid a pall over the crew. They reminded us that the Army was out there—an implacable debt for something you had no choice about buying—and of the precarious dance of deferments that might postpone or cancel payment. You could ignore the draft and take your chances, or order your life around the priority of staying out of it. With adequate grades and straight progress towards a degree, a student deferment was still a sure thing. I wondered whether shifting to forestry, adding two years to my program, would threaten my deferment. My local draft board administered an area where many high school graduates went on to college. They were having a hard time meeting their quota out of the inventory of men that remained.

The bureaucratic grinder could get you, but so could caprice. Five men I knew at Pomona had taken a semester off to work on a community development project in Costa Rica. Two of them had been drafted, the others deferred.

We were sorry that Stinson, Perez, and Moya had been drafted, but relieved that we hadn't been, as though the proximity inoculated us, gave us some sort of immunity. Of the three, Stinson took it hardest. The induction notice left him dazed, frightened. We unrolled our stories— secondhand, at best, for the most part— of how to beat it. Snead said that uppers would boost your blood pressure out of sight, or you could always get nailed for a felony. Kruger recommended adding powdered sugar to your urine sample. Mundeen said there was a doctor in Oakland who could get you out for a price. Jarvis talked about trying to convince them you were queer or crazy. Orem knew about putting in for conscientious objector status, and Calendar about going to Canada. The possibilities buoyed Stinson up a little. Moya chipped in as we broke for lunch.

"Hey, even if you go, it ain't so bad. The army needs some white guys. With all them spooks and spics, you could be a general in no time. Besides, you'll have me there to look out for you. Keep bad hombres like Sunshine from taking advantage."

Stinson laughed.

"See, ain't nothing to it. After working for Cable, killing gooks is gonna be a snap. And all that Chinese pussy. I hear they give you a world cruise for two bucks and a carton of Marlboros."

At lunch, Cable told us we could leave at four-thirty. He told me to stick around after I ate and help Bailey wax the mess hall floor. Bailey finished the dishes while I mopped the floor.

Cable came out of his office, glanced toward the kitchen, and walked over.

"You going into town tonight?"

"Yes." I wondered if he needed someone for late duty.

"You know the Midway Tavern?"

"No. I don't think so."

"It's on Foothill, down from K-Mart. You can't miss it. Stop in and I'll buy you a beer."

"I don't know," I said, puzzled by the invitation. Besides, Kelly wasn't twenty-one and didn't like taverns much anyway.

"It's the only place I can talk without Bailey's ear to the keyhole or the crew thinking something funny's going on. Besides, I get tired of the old lady beating me at pool. You play?"

"Some."

"See you there, then?"

"Sure," I said. I could get around to Kelly later. "What time?"

"Any time you get there."

The Midway turned out to be an overlit, oversized, country-western tavern with topless barmaids and a headache-sized band. Cable was sitting in the back near the pool tables. Raylene was shooting. She missed a tough bank shot as I came up. Raylene wrinkled her nose and backed away from the table.

"Nice try," said the man she was playing. He was blond and stocky, wearing a t-shirt with the sleeves cut off and the words "Rodeo— America's Second Favorite Sport" printed across the front.

She waved when she saw me. "Hi, honey. Put your money up and get a beer from Captain Hook."

The man missed a combination shot and Raylene bent back over the table. Her breasts jogged as she banged in a shot. I put my quarter on the table and sat down with Cable. He poured me a beer and waved the empty pitcher at a barmaid. She was talking to two men and didn't seem to notice.

"Ever since this place went topless, the broads think all they have to do is walk around with their tits flopping. It's getting so you need an act of God to get a beer around here."

The barmaid finally strolled over.

"You want another one, Bobby?"

"You think I was waving this pitcher around to catch flies?"

"How should I know?" She picked up the pitcher and an empty glass.

"You know, Connie," said Cable, "if your brains were half the size of your boobs, it'd be a big improvement. It's too bad they didn't pass out smarts in the same line they passed out tits."

"You think you're so smart." Connie strutted away.

"And bring Raylene another one of those wine gizmos." Cable watched her cross the room. "Jesus, if you could milk those it'd put a herd of cows out of business. Ray's not half bad herself, but Connie. . . ." Cable shook his head.

The band was finishing a set with "Ring of Fire:"

"I fell into a burning ring of fire,
I fell down, down, down,
And the flames leapt higher.
And it burns, burns, burns,
The ring of fire,
The ring of fire."

The band sounded as though they'd met for the first time in the parking lot on the way in. Cable tapped a Camel on his fitting and lit up.

"So, you hear anything about Snead?"

"No," I said. "I don't think he has one though."

Cable shrugged. "I don't think so either, but that don't mean he doesn't." He rubbed his arm where the fitting was joined to it. "I don't care much one way or the other. I just don't like being lied to, and I don't like not knowing what's going on. That's where it makes a difference. I don't like having to do it this way, but times change. I can't just haul him out back and beat on him till I'm sure he's telling me the truth. So I got to do it any way I can. I've seen kids get a hair up their ass when they got a gun. Snead's a chance I'm taking; he's not gonna be a chance the crew has to take."

"Sure," I said.

Cable stopped rubbing his arm and began to twist it slowly back and forth. The metal fitting was laced with nicks and gouges.

"Did, uh, you lose your arm in Korea?"

"Yeah," said Cable. Funny thing is, I wasn't even hit there. They were patching up my stomach in an aid station and pumping me full of oxygen. There must have been a leak because there was a flash fire that burned my arm pretty good before they got to me. I was out cold when it happened, so there was nothing I could do about it. It got infected and they finally had to take it off."

Cable flexed the arm and watched Raylene miss a shot on the eight ball.

"Sometimes it aches like hell and I have to ice it down. The doctors at the V.A. hospital keep telling me not to use it so hard. Hell, you can't fight fire with one arm." Cable mashed out his cigarette. "Last year, I heard about an artificial leg made out of this titanium alloy stuff from the space program. The doctors said they could make me up one out of it, but it would cost me an arm and a leg." Cable laughed at the little joke. "But I been saving up; a few more campaign fires and I'll be trading in my Ford on a Corvette." He rang his empty glass on the fitting.

Connie came back with the pitcher and a glass of wine. She was still pouting, or pretending to. Cable told her to keep the change from the five and she brightened, crooning her thanks.

"Buy yourself a forklift," said Cable as she started away.

She turned, uncertain. "Is that some kind of drink?"

Cable grinned. "Yeah. I can suck them up by the jugfull."

She went on to another table.

"Connie's a good kid. Another month or so, she'll be as hard as the rest of them. Tough way to make a living."

"You're up." Raylene appeared at the table and picked up her drink. "Let's shoot partners."

"How're you doing, Ray?" Cable asked.

"A couple more of these and I'm going to be doing just fine." She took a long swallow.

"Winning any bucks?"

"Enough to keep me honest."

"I taught her everything she knows," said Cable.

"A woman's born knowing all she needs to know. Bobby just reminded me how to use it."

Cable swatted her on the rump.

"How's it feel, Bobby?" Raylene tapped his fitting with her cue.

"All right," said Cable.

"Maybe you ought to soak it."

"Yeah."

We played three games against the blond in the t-shirt named Butch and his partner. The other man was drunk, and we won easily. Raylene played a chancy, aggressive game; I was cautious and steadier. We made a good team. While we were waiting for another challenge, Raylene went to the bathroom and Cable came over.

"I got some stuff to take care of. You mind seeing that Ray gets home?"

"Sure," I said.

Cable spun the cue ball down the table, banking it off three rails into a pocket.

"Eat 'em up, kid," he said, turning away. "See you Thursday."

Raylene and I kept winning. Her nipples showed under her white blouse, and she rubbed against me moving around the table. I began to touch back. We finally lost when Raylene scratched on the eight ball. We sat at a table, waiting for our quarter to come back up. The band sounded better now and Raylene sang along.

"Let's dance," said Raylene, pumping in her chair to the music.

"I'm not very good at it."

"That's OK, I am." She got up. "Besides, like Stumpy says, when you sign on with Uncle, you sign on for other duties as assigned."

She led me out on the floor. After I faked my way through a fast one, she wrapped me up in a long, slow number. Halfway through, I had an erection and she pressed into it.

"I like you," she said, and sang along with the band: "I don't want it to be over, I cannot let you go."

When the dance was over, I went to the bathroom. I used a stall so I wouldn't have to stand in the open at a urinal, still flying my erection. The walls of the stall were crusted with simple obscenities and phone numbers. And above them all, in bold, red ink: "Don't look up here—the joke's in your hand." I thought about Cable and wondered how far Raylene or I would be willing to take it. I thought, too, about Mundeen's warning at the party.

Raylene had her sweater on when I got back to the table. She squeezed my thigh under the table.

"Sorry, lover, but something's come up." She moved her hand up my thigh and squeezed again. "Some other time, OK?"

"Sure," I said, a little sullen.

"Hey," she said, "I say what I mean. If I wanted to play pricktease, I'd go back to high school." Raylene picked up her purse. "I got to go."

"See you," I said.

"If you can't keep it hard, keep it handy." She wound her way among the dancers and went out the door with Butch.

Connie came by after a while and I ordered another pitcher.

"You a friend of Bobby's?" she asked when she came back.

"Sort of," I said.

"What does that mean?"

"I work for him."

"Oh, you're a fireman."

"That's right," I said, getting interested. "You worked here long?" I had enough beer in me that I didn't have any trouble looking right at her whopping foreground.

"Well, when you see him, tell him I figured out his little forklift joke and I got something to tell him the next time he comes in."

"I'll tell him," I said. "Would you like to go out for a drink or something when you're done here?"

"No," she said, and walked away.

The band was playing "Ring of Fire" again. The singer sounded like Johnny Cash with a mouthful of vaseline. I left.

In the parking lot, I sat in my car for a while. When I called Kelly earlier in the evening, no one was home. I hadn't seen her since the party. Mundeen had gone in one night after standby. He said I was wrecking his home life; all Karen would do was go on about what a jerk I was. Kelly wouldn't come out of her room.

I drove past her house and parked across the street. There was a light in the kitchen, but the rest of the rooms were dark. Kelly's car was in the driveway. I rang the doorbell and waited. I was on my way back to the car when she opened the door.

"Hi," she said.

"Hello." I turned back and went up the steps. Kelly stayed in the doorway.

"I'd like to go out and get some coffee," she said.

"You go out drinking with strangers, ma'am?" It was the wrong thing to say.

"My life would be a lot easier if I didn't."

"Ok," I said, "let's get some coffee." With that kind of start, it was going to be a long way around to bed, if we got there at all. I was starting to lose the fluent edge from the beer, and wondered whether I could manage the accusations and explanations that were going to be a requisite for spending the night.

We drove to one of those all-night, fluorescent coffee shops. Kelly's face looked gray in the eye-watering expanse of pastel, day-glo plastic. We both ordered coffee. I tried to call up the soft caving that came to me from Kelly's scalloped scar and the wonderful coppery ruff farther down.

"How've you been?" I asked, trying to get what I could of the caving into my voice.

"Why should you care?"

"Look," I said, "I'm sorry. We just haven't had any days off."

"Mike managed to come in."

"Yeah." I wasn't sure where to go from there. I hadn't come in because I knew Kelly would go back to work on me with her kitchen table tarot readings, her questions and warnings. Since the party, things had become more complicated. I didn't want her persistence and my own doubts to work me, flat-footed, into a corner and coerce some arbitrary, premature resolution.

"I just needed some time to myself," I said.

"Maybe you want the rest of your life to yourself."

"Look. I wanted to sort some things out, and I figured I could do it better up there. That's all."

I took a swallow of coffee. Kelly hadn't touched hers.

"You look. You've had all summer to think about things. All I hear about are 'ambivalencies' and 'incongruities' and the rest of that intellectual bullshit you hide out in whenever something tough comes up. You don't listen to me; you don't even talk to me. You think I'm a piece of candy you can pop in your mouth any time you roll into town. Well let me tell you, cowboy, that's not the way it works. Just because I don't go to your expensive college doesn't mean I'm stupid, so you can stop treating me like I was." Kelly stopped to gather herself. I wondered how spontaneous this all was.

"What I'm telling you is the truth, whether you want to hear it or not. If you don't have that in a relationship, you don't have anything."

"Are you talking about us or about tarot truth?"

"Both. They're part of the same thing."

"I'm sorry, but I just can't see running a relationship according to how a deck of cards happens to get shuffled."

"There you go again. That's not fair, David. The tarot doesn't run anything—it suggests tendencies, some strong, some not. And sometimes you can't make anything out at all. But you tell me, just look at me and tell me, that something weird isn't going on at Dalton."

Kelly's voice was full of confidence in the accusation. I looked up from my coffee.

"I can't tell you that," I said, after what seemed a long time, "because I don't know."

She slumped a little, but her voice was still strong.

"You know," she said. "I can tell. You won't admit it because you can't figure it all out, but you know. You don't have to understand everything before it can be true."

"If we're going to get into the philosophy of perception— "

"Don't hide out on me again. This isn't some college greenhouse. This is real life where things happen to people."

"What do you want me to do—tell Cable that he's got a crazy Indian and a simpleton with nightmares and some other odds and ends that are making things tough on poor Davey and that my girlfriend who does card tricks wants him to make everyone promise to cut it out?"

"I want you to quit."

"You mean move out of your house of cards? How are you going to know how things turn out if I don't stick around to call your bet? Or don't you want to know?"

"I already know," said Kelly quietly. "That's why I want you to get out."

"Well, that's easy. Why don't you just tell me what's going to happen. If I don't think I can handle it, I'll pack it in."

"Someone's going to die."

"Oh bullshit. Don't you think this has gone far enough?"

"I don't want it to have to."

I let out a long sigh and spoke with deliberate patience.

"Have you ever predicted somebody's death before?"

"No."

"What makes you think you can do something like that?"

"If I wasn't sure, I wouldn't tell you." Kelly's voice was sad, but firm. I couldn't think of any way to talk her out of it. Only the future could do that.

"What difference would quitting make?"

"You'd be safe. Maybe it would change things."

We sat without speaking for a while.

"What are you going to do?"

"Take you home, I guess."

"David, I can't keep seeing you if you don't quit."

"I'm sorry," I said, "I can't do that."

We drove back to her house. I parked in front with the engine running.

"Please?"

I shook my head. "I'll call you when the season's over."

Kelly opened the door and ran into the house. I drove back to Dalton, tired, sad, a little angry.

In the morning, I sat with Speyer who was eating breakfast alone. Calendar and Perez hadn't come in yet. Moya wasn't there either. Speyer ate fastidiously, using his napkin often. I asked if he knew anything about the tarot.

"A little," he said. "I don't think it's much different from any other kind of fortune telling."

"Do you think there's anything to it?"

"I doubt it." He pruned the hard, greasy edge from his fried egg. "Some personality types are prone to the neurosis that they can predict events. It seems to confirm for them that although their life—everybody's life—is largely out of our hands, we can still cut corners, swindle the future. Once they have that established, they can structure their hunches and construe outcomes so that their predictions become self-verifying. There's a good living to be made at it if you have a little flair. Of course, there are people who genuinely believe in that sort of thing." Speyer took a small sip of coffee.

"For instance, I'm sure Jimmy really thinks he can divine the world by mutilating lizards. And he's certainly more interesting than your ordinary crystal ball fondler or table thumper. Here, he's a cultural relic, but I'd guess on whatever reservation he comes from there's still a support system of believers. It's a good deal easier to be sincere when you're believed in at least some of the time."

"Did he do that to the lizard?"

"I'm sure he did."

"Did you ask him?"

Speyer smiled at me quizzically. "No."

Speyer pushed some hominy onto his fork with his knife. "How did you come to your interest in the tarot?"

"Oh, there's a girl I know who does readings. It's got her messed up to the point where she runs her life by the cards."

"I wouldn't worry too much about it. Sometimes it's a phase people go through—like stamp collecting."

"Maybe," I said. "I hope so."

Cable stopped me on my way out of the mess hall.

"How'd your luck run?"

"We won quite a few games after you left," I said uneasily.

"I figured you must have. Ray came in late doing her jackpot number. One of these times I just might pack it in and let her support me."

"She shoots a good stick."

"Yeah," said Cable, "and she gets better all the time. Everything else is starting to sag a little, but her game just keeps getting tighter. If you ever get married, find yourself a moneymaker. She'll keep you interested after her ass is loose as an old shoe."

Calendar and Perez still hadn't come in when we finished the obstacle course. Moya had called in sick. The rules had been laid down at the start of the season. If you didn't show up and you hadn't called in, you were gone. Cable sent us into the mess hall and asked about Perez and Calendar.

"Maybe they got a better offer from the city zoo," said Mundeen.

Kruger brayed in laughter. "About time somebody put Calendar where he belongs."

"Cut it," said Cable. "Does anybody know anything about it?"

"They will not come back." Jimmy was standing near the doorway. "They took what they had and they will not come back."

"Their gear's gone?" Cable asked.

Jimmy nodded.

"Shit," said Stinson, "Perez owes me five."

"Let's go to work," said Cable, walking rigidly down the room.

We spent the day cutting a firebreak between a parking area for a viewpoint and a steep brushfield below it. At lunch, Stonecrofter complained about a rash.

"It's probably syph," said Kruger. "But there's nothing to worry about until your prick falls off. Not that anybody would be able to tell the difference."

Halfway through the afternoon, Stonecrofter threw down his McLeod.

"Shit! I can't stand it. I got to do something."

Cable came back down the line. Stonecrofter was rubbing his chest fiercely. He unbuttoned his shirt and Cable took a look.

"It's oak," he said. "Goddamnit, what do you think those drops are for?"

"I take them every day," Stonecrofter said sullenly.

At the start of the season, we'd each been issued a vile of poison oak vaccine. A few drops every day were supposed to provide immunity to poison oak. The taste was so bad, even diluted in a glass of milk, that most of us stopped using it.

Stonecrofter's skin was inflamed with boils, running from his throat down past his navel.

"I just noticed it yesterday a little bit on my neck. I don't know where I got into it."

"There was a patch that burned on Skyhook. You don't have to touch it to catch it. Your pores open up when you sweat and the smoke carries the shit right in." Cable shook his head. "Where you got it, the sweat's gonna run it on down to where you're gonna wish you was dead."

Nelson looked down in fear, getting the idea.

"He's safe," said Kruger. "Nelly ain't sweated all summer."

"What do I do?"

"Cominsky, you still got any of that stuff?"

"I think so, Bob. I think I got some in the barracks."

When we got back, Cominsky dragged a trunk from under his bunk and dug around in it. The trunk was crammed with tubes, bottles, and jars.

"Jesus," said Mundeen, "it looks like a drugstore in there. You use all that stuff for your bald spot?"

Cominsky laughed. "Naw. This is mostly left over from when the wife and me was distributors for Vita-Glo. We went broke doing it, and she won't let me keep any of this around the house. Says it reminds her of that. You can never tell when it'll come in handy though. Like this wart remover—it's great stuff. You oughta try some."

"We should try the whole jar on Nelly's head," said Kruger.

"Here we are." Cominsky opened a small box and shook out some turquoise cubes. "Copper sulfate."

"How does it work?" asked Stonecrofter.

"Beats me," said Cominsky, "but it does the job."

"I mean, how do you use it?"

"Well, you grind it up with a little water and make a paste and spread it on. It burns like hell, but it dries the oak right up."

"I don't care if it hurts. This stuff is killing me."

Cominsky made the salve and gave it to Stonecrofter. "Go to it."

Stonecrofter dabbed a little on.

"Naw, you gotta lay it on thick. It don't work otherwise."

Nelson smeared on all the paste. He sat on his bunk, waiting. "This doesn't feel so bad."

"It will," said Cominsky.

Ten minutes later, Stonecrofter was walking back and forth in the room, twisting his torso. "Oh shit, oh fuck, oh shit fuck screw."

"Listen to the mouth on that boy." Most of us were amused, but sympathetic. For Kruger, the spectacle was pure enjoyment. "Cominsky, you got a bar of soap in there for Nelly's mouth?"

"Can't I wash it off?" Stonecrofter pleaded.

"Not if you want it to do any good. It's got to stay on at least a half an hour."

"I can't stand it," said Nelson, wheeling into another lap of the bunkhouse.

"Hey," said Kruger, nudging Mundeen. "I can fix it for you so you'll hardly notice."

"How?" asked Stonecrofter, dubious but desperate.

"Come here."

Stonecrofter walked up. Kruger waved his hand. "Right up next to me here." Nelson edged closer.

"It hurts like hell, right?"

Stonecrofter nodded.

"And you'd do anything to make it stop?"

"Well. . ." Stonecrofter nodded again.

"Don't do it." Snead spoke flatly.

"What do you mean?" Kruger's face clouded as he turned toward Snead.

"I said leave him alone. The poor fucker's hurting enough already."

Stonecrofter jumped back. "What was he going to do to me?"

"Aw, he was gonna boot you in the shins or thump your nuts or something and then ask if you still noticed how much that goop was hurting you."

Kruger started to say something, but checked it before any words got out. Even Mundeen was careful not to push Snead very far. Kruger was bigger than Snead by forty pounds or so, but there was the clear sense that if it came down to it, Snead was capable of anything in a fight. Even if Kruger won, he was going to get hurt.

"What a bunch of babies. Shit." Kruger got up and walked out.

Moya came in the next morning. He talked to Cable briefly in the office. On our way to the obstacle course, Stinson asked what happened to Perez. Moya shrugged.

"He decided not to work here anymore."

"Calendar too?"

"I don't know nothing about Calendar."

That evening after supper, I needed to shake off the blunt heat in the flat. I headed up the ridge, aiming for the grove I had found earlier. The sun was still an hour or so above the mountains, but the breeze along the ridgeline eased the friction of the heat. In the grove, I smoked and looked back to the flat, the compound a child's model of itself. Above me, the pitch of the ridge increased, passing into a transitional zone that led on to the cathedral scarps of the Santa Sangres. Restless, a little curious for wilder country, I headed up. The climbing was steeper now, and some quirk in the atmosphere had sealed an envelope of heat as heavy as the air in the flat and dense with moisture. The ridge ended in a rock headwall that came down like a prow. I went west along the base of the bluff, weaving through a luxuriant field of manzanita, tall and richly green at this better-watered altitude. Farther on, the manzanita was ruptured by a great rockfall. I worked my way over the massive slabs of rock, poised like a wreckage of boxcars, each piece seeming the linchpin that held the whole slide in place. I came out on a little bench and stopped to let the heaviness and small tremors pass out of my legs; on the way back, I would loop below the slide. I pulled out a cigarette, but held it unlit, tilting my head and looking hard, as I caught odd, shuffling noises and snatches of sound like wind through wire. The sounds came from below me and farther along the bluff, from a second bench that stairstepped off from where I stood. I went gingerly on through the manzanita, trying to match the sounds with anything in my inventory, and came suddenly onto a narrow avenue of sight that stiffened me into a throat-clinching crouch. Across the bench and a little below me, not fifty feet away, Jimmy danced in a cleared circle in the brush. Except it was not a dance. Feinting, dipping in nimble lunges and back, circling counterclockwise, Jimmy wielded his hook, carving the air. He was barefoot, naked except for pale buckskin pants and his belt. The circle was marked at four points on its perimeter with a bundle of sticks, each with a topknot of feathers. The air was smudged with dust, and in the jaundiced light it settled on his torso, banking the shimmering sweat. A samurai at practice. Except it was not a drill.

His dodging flinches, his absolute attention, the run of continuous and muted keening that rose from him: beyond question, Jimmy faced an opponent as real to him as death. Then a liquid move clockwise and a deeper lunge, a hissing upsweep of the hook that jolted mid-stroke as though it had passed through solid flesh. Jimmy backed and came forward again, poised, staring down; the hook flashing then in a great circle above his head and one pillar of sound "Waagh!" as the hook slipped from his grasp and spun into the brush beyond the ring. Jimmy jumped back again, into a bandy crouch, circling once more, working his way toward the center and finally closing on it, holding the air in a grip that braided the muscles in his arms and shoulders and shook his body. Finally, his legs buckled and he went down, thrashing and rolling across the circle into the brush. He lay on his back: still, then twitching, then bucking in spasms as fierce as his motions in the clearing but now plainly unwilled. Drool ran down out of both sides of his mouth and his eyes rolled back, leaving a yellow-white membrane in the sockets. At last he went limp. His eyelids closed, and a dark stain began to spread across the crotch of his pants.

I waited in ice until his breathing was nearly regular, then crept back, feeling behind me with my hands, watching till the brush closed me off. Back to the far side of the bench, I turned down the slope, beating through the brush below the rockfall in a clumsy skid until I came on a deer trail and jogged back to the ridge. I tried to remember what I knew about epileptic seizures. Jimmy had not bitten his tongue—there was no red in his drool—and his even breathing meant he hadn't choked on it. He would wake up—was already awake—and would be all right. The bizarre charade in the clearing must have triggered the fit—maybe, yes, was an early stage of it.

And farther down, Dalton rising out of the flat like home, I understood that this was what I had needed to center Jimmy. His exotic monologues must have been the harvest of years of seizures.

Once I was able to place him in that framework, Jimmy's apparent radical difference domesticated into the quirks of blood chemistry and wayward electrical pulses in the brain. While this might not explain him altogether, it closed the deeper fractures of uncertainty he had laid open in me. I slept easily that night, and without dreams.

In the morning, Jimmy looked placid, almost serene. We didn't go out on project work that day. Instead, Cable had us do a scrub and polish job on all the buildings in the compound. I was assigned to the tool shed with Mundeen and Cominsky. There wasn't much to do. Cable demanded that the tool room be kept in order on a day-to-day basis. After we swept up and cleaned the windows, we puttered away the morning sharpening some project tools. Mundeen asked if I'd seen Kelly on my day off.

"Yeah, we had a talk."

"So? You get things worked out?"

"I guess so. We aren't going to be seeing each other."

"Jesus." Mundeen put down the pulaski he was working on. "You got any idea what this is doing to my love life? Listen, Karen's a regular pinball machine in bed—you put in whatever's handiest and all her lights go on and her bells go off. It's like a goddamn carnival. And every time she makes it, she starts sneezing. I never seen anything like it. Lately, she hasn't even puckered her nose, and if she gets that hair another inch up her ass she's liable to cut me off altogether just because I'm a friend of yours."

I grinned. "Maybe you could go back to bowling balls. Anyway, I heard sex is bad for athletes—saps all those precious bodily fluids; milks the mean right out of you."

Mundeen rolled his eyes. "What'd you mean—look at Cominsky. He hasn't got any in months and look at the shape he's in."

Cominsky shook his head. "Someday when you cockhounds get married you're gonna find out what sex is really like."

"Give us a break, Cominsky. Let us in on the secret."

Cominsky thought about it. "Well, when you start out, it's sort of like good, sharp cheddar cheese."

"It always tasted like fish to me," said Mundeen.

"But after while it sort of loses that edge, you know, and it gets to be more like Velveeta. That's when you got to have other interests to keep you occupied."

"You got some little interest on the side that keeps you occupied?" Mundeen tapped Cominsky's shoulder with his knuckles.

"Naw, I don't run around. I mean something like television or a hobby or something."

"Jesus," said Mundeen, "I can hardly wait. Being married sounds like more fun than a night in the library."

"You'll see. That's just the way things are. Sex isn't everything."

Mundeen snorted. "It sure has got whatever's in second place beat by six inches."

We went back to working on the tools. Just before lunch, we ran out of wax for the handles. Cominsky thought there might be an old can of it in the utility shed. I lost the coin flip and went down to look for it. I hadn't been back since I found the pistol. Snead had enough chances to get rid of it by now. Maybe it wasn't even his. It could have been left by someone else, some other season even. Pitkin and Stonecrofter were working in the shed. Nelson came out as I walked up.

"How's the oak?"

"That stuff really works. It hardly itches at all now, and it isn't spreading anymore." He walked off toward the mess hall with a mop and bucket.

Dick was inside, putting some stray electrical parts into a box, humming to himself.

"How's it going?" I glanced up, looking for the bag. A half sheet of plywood was propped against the wall, partially shielding the spot where the bag had been.

"Hi, David. Everything's going pretty good." He waved his arm around. "Except I can't figure out though how Mr. Cable ever let this place get like this. It's gonna take a lot of work."

"Looks like. Say, have you come across a can of wax?" I moved along the wall to where I could get a clear view behind the plywood.

"No. Do you want me to look for it?"

"I guess we could poke around." I started by moving the plywood. The bag wasn't in sight. While Dick sorted through the contents of a cardboard box, I reached up and skimmed my fingers along the unfinished space. Nothing.

Dick started humming again as we looked for the wax. The honest pleasure he took in detail work had astonished me early in the season. As I watched, I realized that this quality had come back into him. For several weeks, he had been increasingly mechanical, almost inanimate. I felt guilty about avoiding that fact, especially since I felt partly responsible, through Kelly, for provoking his problems.

"Been sleeping better?"

"A lot better." Dick had a small hitch in his voice. Then he grinned. "Real good."

"That's great. No more dreams?"

Dick shook his head. "No, I just go to sleep now."

I found a tin of wax and pried it open. The wax was hard and fractured as a dry lake bed. I pitched it in a trash box and turned to leave.

"I still dream," said Dick, "except it's different now. Jimmy gave me some stuff you can make like tea and I drink one cup every night. When I start to dream it now, I can make it not happen. I can get out of the dream."

"Did you tell Jimmy about your dream?"

"No. Not exactly. I mean, he sort of just knew about it anyway."

I nodded and started back for the tool shed.

"Hey." Dick was in the doorway, excited. "I wanted to tell you. I beat Mr. Jacobs two times in a row last week. I never done that before. You and your girlfriend come down sometime and I'll take you around. They give me a special price."

Mundeen was talking about Calendar when I got back.

"You know, I never could figure him out. He was all right on the line, but he hated doing this kind of work. I could see him splitting, because I could never see him here in the first place."

"Maybe he needed the job," said Cominsky.

"Shit, nobody needs this job unless he's getting something more out of it than money."

"Sure," I said, "like me—I'm in it for the intellectual challenge and for all the glory and women."

"Hey," said Mundeen, "that reminds me. I heard there's a lady on a tanker crew somewhere up on the Los Padres. Wouldn't that be sweet? She's probably a real dog though. Who else would want that kind of job?"

"Aw," said Cominsky, "I don't believe it."

"No shit. A friend of mine saw her on a fire."

"It's not natural."

"Most natural thing in the world."

"Sure," said Cominsky, "that's all we need around here. We'd be out beating the brush for the crew every time we had to roll. Don't you ever let up thinking about that stuff?"

"Never up, never in."

Bailey hollered from the mess hall and we broke for lunch. Cable came out of his office as we walked in. Oscar was with him.

Before we ate, Cable told everyone to stick around after lunch. Bailey had put together one of his best meals. Nothing was scorched, soggy, or underdone. Mundeen shoveled another load of potatoes onto his plate.

"We ought to invite the ranger up more often. This stuff tastes damn near like food."

"Just like the Last Supper," said Stinson. "I'll bet they've got some real good deal lined up for us."

"Sure," said Jarvis, "they're going to make us all GS-5's and give us a week off at the beach.

After we'd finished eating, Cable spoke above our clatter.

"Ok, listen up. The ranger here has got some things he wants to say."

Oscar walked to the front of the room. His uniform was rumpled, and he had some of Bailey's gravy on his shirt.

"Like Bob said, there are a few things I'd like to go over with you. I don't get up here as often as I should, so I'll be glad to hear any questions I can help out with." Oscar pulled up a chair and straddled it, arms folded across its back.

"First of all, I want you to know I've been keeping track of the kind of work you've been doing. I expect a lot from Dalton, and you've delivered. Dalton's had a fine reputation for a long time, and you're part of that reputation now. As far as I'm concerned, Dalton sets the standard for fire crews. You're the best on this Forest, and there's no tougher fire country than the Santa Sangres to measure a crew by. I think that's something you can be proud of— both as part of a team and as individuals."

"I know most of you won't end up with the Forest Service, but what you learn here can make you the kind of men who can do a job for anybody. For those of you who stay on with the Forest Service, this will give you an idea of how much to expect from yourself and anyone who works for you—not just in fire control but in any branch of forest management. I just want to tell you all again what a fine job you've been doing."

Oscar cleared his throat and looked around. "Mind if I have one of those?" He pointed to a pack of cigarette on the table in front of me. I started to bring them to him, but he motioned me down.

"Just pitch me one." He caught the cigarette deftly and lit it. "My wife's been after me to quit. So far I've managed to quit smoking my own." Oscar took a greedy drag and let the smoke linger in his lungs.

"The other thing I wanted to bring you up to date on is our status at this point in the season. I understand you just lost two men, and we're going to try to do something about that. Frankly, I'm not optimistic. It's hard to get the kind of men we need to do the job, but Dalton was already three men under its authorized manning and this concerns me. I don't want to see us out on a limb because we're caught short. Over the long haul, we're in pretty fair shape. The Northwest has been having a wet summer, so we should be able to pull in crews and jumpers from Region 6 if we get in a real bind. But I'm still going to do everything I can to fill those slots."

"Now, what we're looking at for the rest of the season is a combination of factors that's not going to make life any easier for any of us. You all know what the weather's been like. What you may not know is that we've been in a drying trend for three years now. That means that not only the fine and medium fuels are dried out, but the big stuff, something we call the one hundred hour time-lag fuels have lost a lot of moisture. They're going to catch quicker, and they're going to burn hotter and longer. Then there's the California Oaks. You might have noticed a lot of them don't have any live foliage. We had two killer frosts in May after the leaves were out. What that left us with is a lot of flash fuel up in the canopy. I don't have to tell you how dangerous that can be. And to top it off, we're moving into Santa Ana season. Our meteorologists don't expect it to be severe, but any of you who've fought fire in a Santa Ana wind know that severe is a relative term. Any Santa Ana fire is going to be a bad one."

Oscar stubbed out his cigarette. "Bob, is there anything else?"

Cable pushed back his chair. "Like the ranger said, it's not gonna get any easier, but whatever it takes to get the job done, that's what we're gonna do and we'll do it with what we've got on board. I wouldn't trade any one of you for three rookie Mundeens. And about the kind of work you've been doing. Don't get too swelled up. What you did is what needed to be done. That doesn't mean you can't do more of it, and do it better."

Oscar waited, but Cable was through.

"Are there any questions?"

Pitkin stood up. "Can anybody get a career like you said with the Forest Service if they really want to?"

Oscar pushed out his lips and drew a finger across them. "I'll tell you, Dick, a lot of that has to do with the Civil Service Commission. It's not entirely up to us. Why don't you stop by the station on one of your days off and I can fill you in on the whole business. That'll give me a chance to dig up the information you need. Just tell my secretary you have an appointment and come on in."

"Sure thing." Dick sat down, grinning.

"Anything else?"

"Does the Forest Service plan to continue its even-flow, sustained yield timber policy?" Jarvis leaned forward intently.

"Who gives a rat's ass?" Kruger muttered under his breath.

"That's a tough one. It's a political issue as much as a matter of forest practices. Why don't you stick around after we're through and I'll tell you what I know about it. It's mainly a Region 6 concern, but with some of the new logging systems coming on line, we may be able to get at some ground that was unloggable ten years ago. That could change the whole picture."

There were no more questions and we went back to work.

Later in the afternoon, Speyer came by the tool shed. Cable had told him to take someone up with him and reanchor the pipe on the obstacle course. Mundeen had shaken it loose going across that morning. Speyer asked if I wanted to go along.

We walked up the course, dust puffing around us where the dirt had been milled by the crew's boots. By the time we reached the draw, we were coated from the waist down with a gray pall of powder. The pipe didn't look to be hard to fix. Some nuts had loosened where a crossbar on the pipe bolted into an angle iron frame. Speyer cinched the nuts down with a pipe wrench he had brought. One of the bolts had lost its nut and slipped out of its hole. I sifted through the dirt and came up with the nut. Without the bolt in place, the crosspiece sagged a fraction and the bolt wouldn't fit back in. I tried to raise the pipe to line up the holes. Even lying on my back, feet planted against the pipe, trying to lift with my legs, I couldn't move it. We couldn't lift together because one of us would have to pound the bolt in when there was enough clearance.

"I could go back and get a couple of the guys or maybe the jack from the truck."

"Let's see if I can't save you the hike." Speyer crouched under the pipe, pressing his shoulders into it and grasping the metal with both hands. He moved against it and the pipe lifted. I slid the bolt home free.

Speyer straightened. "It's mostly a matter of leverage. If you get the angle right, you can move more than you'd think."

"A little muscle to lever with doesn't hurt any." That Speyer had raised the pipe surprised me some; that he had done it without apparent strain surprised me a lot.

"True enough." He smiled. "I used to do isometrics. They're not only good for strength, but for attitude. When you practice against something that's immobile, it's easier to imagine movement in something that's susceptible to it."

I sat down on the support and lit a cigarette.

"What do you think about what Oscar had to say? Did you notice how Cable, I don't know, backhanded him about getting some new men and about the kind of job we've done?"

"Yes," said Speyer, "but you have to understand that Bob and Oscar are fundamentally two quite different kinds of men."

"Sure, I can see that."

"Which of course leads them to take different approaches in managing men. Oscar is a synthesizer. He'll accept what he's given to work with and blend it toward a goal, but he won't tamper with a person's shape in doing it. It requires a lot of attention and a delicate hand to operate that way. Bob can't work that way. He takes what he has and tries to make it what he wants. He's only comfortable with an instrument he's hammered out for himself. That's why he's largely made Dalton into an extension of his will."

"I'd never thought of it like that. It makes sense, though. Both ways seem to work."

Speyer moistened his lips with his tongue.

"They do, depending on the context. And I'm afraid that Bob is running out of context."

"How?"

"Well, as Bob would put it, five years ago he could say 'jump' and the crew would ask 'how high?' They still jump, but now they're asking themselves why. This year, or the next, or the one after that, they're going to start asking Bob. America made men like Cable and then changed out from under them. There's less and less of Bob's kind of coercion around, and he's going to find it harder every season to field a crew who will accommodate it."

"But there has to be discipline to hold it all together. Somebody has to take charge."

"Discipline and coercion are not the same. Coercion is discipline's dark side. Coercion is external—subject to abuse and, theoretically, at least in America, dependent on the acquiescence of those it's applied to. Real discipline is internal. It works because it frees you from distraction. You can concentrate completely on what you want to accomplish. Its success is contingent only on individual character, not intimidation."

Speyer had been speaking quietly, but insistently. He stopped and made a small gesture of disparagement. "You take your chances when you ask me a question. I sometimes wonder if I don't have more ideas about things than there are things to have ideas about."

"You could pass for a professor of something," I said. "The only difference is you're generally interesting."

"Not so generally, I'm afraid. In any case, it's the trained mind at free play, the ideas themselves that warrant our interest. Given a certain level of competence, their expression is incidental. Mind you, rhetoric can give you range beyond your competence and access to careless thinkers. It's a sport I find less resistible than I should."

"How did you ever get into this kind of work, anyway?"

"What would you think if I said that fire is an ancient element, that the soul of man is a work of fire, and that I have been summoned here, now, to stand at the source of my being?" He laughed mildly and answered himself. "I'd say that's what comes of reading too much poetry. No, I'm here largely because I'm lazy. Without this kind of use, my body would go to seed in no time. Then too, I've worked for the Forest Service before. It's somewhat like the Catholic Church in that respect—no matter how great your lapses, they're always willing to take you back into the flock."

Bailey's lunch settled a comfortable notch lower in my stomach.

"How do you keep your mind alive up here? I mean, books can only take you so far."

"I go one-on-one with myself; that keeps me limber enough. It's rather like isometrics: it gives me absolute dimension. I can test myself without limits."

"Where did you go to college?"

"Abroad, mostly."

"You must have done other things for a living."

"Yes. I expect I'll do other things again."

I swung across the pipe to try out our repairs, and we started back down the hill.

"What do you think of the crew? I mean, how does it stack up against other crews you've seen?"

"Offhand, I can't remember a crew that could match it. In terms of individuals, it's not that distinct. A few outlaws, a couple of athletes, one or two career types, some machismo problems, those who just wandered into it. And the same seduction undergirding it for all of us—a chance to walk the edge, tickled by the immensity that would claim us if it could. A *Bildungsroman* for the unwitting; their inadvertent apprenticeship. Rather a standard text, I suppose, with a typical inventory of characters."

"Maybe it's because this is my first crew, but Dalton seems, I don't know, well, special. The chemistry of all this just feels different than anything I've ever been part of."

"Well then, let's see if we can turn up something a bit more resplendent. Have you read Moby Dick?"

"A couple years ago."

"Try this out, then. Here we are on the Dalton-Pequod, sailing the Santa Sangres after the Great White Fire, commanded by Captain Cable, peg arm and all. Jimmy, for example, would be Ahab's cryptic harpooner, Fedallah. Pitkin might be Pip. You could probably work out some other correspondences with a little imagination."

"And some rereading. I kept bogging down in the how-to-run-a-whaler chapters. Some of it's sort of slipped away from me. Who would you be?"

"It's immodest to characterize oneself."

"What about me, then?"

"That's hard to say. Perhaps neither of us fits in. The notion that life imitates art can only be stretched so far."

We dropped down into a notch in the ridge. A jackrabbit broke from a thicket and zigzagged away uphill. I felt easy enough with Speyer now to ask finally what I needed to know. The need was less urgent since I had witnessed Jimmy's seizure—which I had no intention of telling anyone about—but I still wanted to hear what Speyer had to say about Jimmy.

"What does, uh, Jimmy have against you?"

Speyer didn't answer right away. We reached the bottom of the notch and started up the other side. I wondered if I'd pushed too far.

"I mean, why do you think he's so set against you?"

"That's something I've puzzled over a good deal. No one enjoys being hated, especially for no obvious reason." He spoke slowly. "As nearly as I can sort out, he's fixed me as some mythical emblem in his arcane view of the world. Just what, I have no idea. However it is that he sees me, I think it has mostly to do with him and very little to do with me. I believe the clinical term is projection."

We cleared the top and came back into view of the station. The truck was pulled out of its shed and figures crossed the compound, running. We plunged down the ridge as the siren called us back.

We rolled out of the station as soon as Speyer and I climbed into the truck. Mundeen said the fire was somewhere up Bouquet Canyon. Most of the terrain in the Santa Sangres was extreme, but Bouquet Canyon had some of the worst. We'd cut practice line there once; I wasn't looking forward to going back to do it for real.

The canyon was an hour from Dalton over slow roads. We listened to radio traffic on the outside speaker mounted behind the cab. Two new fires were reported, and the initial attack ground tanker on the Bouquet Fire was requesting retardant drops from air tankers. The Forest dispatcher called Cable and asked him to take the license plates of any cars that passed us on the way in and to keep an eye out on the line for evidence of arson.

Five miles from the fire, we could see a mammoth convection column of smoke ballooning over the ridge. A lead plane disappeared into the column, followed by a B-17. Cable switched the radio transmitter into the speaker.

"Cinch up your jock straps. You're gonna earn your money on this one." His voice crackled with anticipation.

"I'll bet he's up there jacking off," said Kruger.

"So what," said Snead. "He's been jacking us off all summer."

"What do you think, Pits? You think big Bob is up there playing a tune on his skin flute?" Kruger leaned back and spit out a wad of gum.

"You guys don't know what you're talking about." Pitkin reddened. "Mr. Cable knows what he's doing."

Kruger snorted a laugh. "I hope he knows enough not to use his left hand."

We turned off the highway and made our way up a jarring fire road into the canyon. The one lane dirt track was cramped between the dry creek bed and canyon wall. Rounding a turn, we looked ahead as the upper end of the canyon came into view, a seething sheet of flame spread across it. Oily creosote smoke boiled up in black eruptions across the burning brushfield and streamed out into the paler convection column. Three pumpers were holding the fire from backing down the canyon. We were the first ground crew there. As we pulled in, the lead plane picked up a PBY and guided it down to a ridge-hugging level. The lead plane wagged its wings and veered away. The PBY lumbered in, barely above stall speed, indistinct in the smoke. It cut loose its load of day-glo magenta bentonite and wound its engines to a high pitch, wallowing out of the smoke in a ponderous climb.

Cable talked to the spotter in the lead plane as we tooled up. By cutting a line across a saddle between rock outcrops on the northeast flank, there was a chance we could turn the fire back from a major drainage to the east. Cable radioed his plan to the supervisor's office and told them to gear up for a campaign fire. We waited while Cable made sure the tanker crews could hold their wet line below where we'd be going up. Two more loads of retardant came in, and another ground tanker.

"China Hat must have got lost," said Stinson.

The fire was on the Newhall, China Hat's district.

"What do you expect when they're sucking one thumb and have the other stuck up their ass?" said Kruger.

"They won't be here," said Cominsky. "The dispatcher rolled them on another fire somewhere up by El Cajon."

"I hope they don't get their shirts dirty," said Mundeen. "We get the barnburner, they get the barbecue. I guess Uncle knows what to do with turkeys after all."

Skirting the fire, we worked our way up, around the base of a bluff and along the spine of a spur ridge to the saddle. From the saddle, we could see the fire fingering down the back side of Bouquet Ridge. By the time it reached the bottom, the brush facing it beneath our saddle would be pre-heated; the fire would be coming up the hill like a freight train full out.

This was the first time all season we had cut indirect line. Oddly enough, hot or direct line was safer. Right on top of the fire, one foot in the black, you flex with its shifts and keep track. As the brush burned out against your line, you worked with the assurance that fire wouldn't cross behind you. As Cable said, if you want to handle a snake you go for the neck, not the tail.

Removed from the heat and smoke, indirect line was easier to cut. But it was challenged simultaneously along its whole length when the fire rolled in. Like a dike in the path of a flash flood, the line had to hold everywhere at once.

The distance through the saddle between the two rock bluffs was less than a quarter mile. We cut an exceptionally wide line, eight to ten feet, along the crest of the saddle and carried it over the back side.

Cable had been calling for retardant drops to back up our line, but the air tankers were spread thin with other priorities and a forty-five minute turnaround. The fire had already started to cook up out of the bottom when we got our only drop. We scrambled off the crest of the saddle and flattened out away from large, loose rocks, tools hugged to our sides and chinstraps securing our hard hats, facing the oncoming B-17. The plane came in at two hundred feet or so, then sagged to less than half that height above the saddle.

"Get up, you bastard! Get it up!" Cable screamed into the radio as 2,000 gallons of retardant poured out.

At that altitude, the bentonite couldn't spread into a fine mist that coated wide swaths of brush. It ploughed into the ground in a solid body. The B-17 banked away, and we climbed back to the saddle. Down the ridge from the center of our line, the retardant had bulldozed a hundred feet of brush into an ominous, dripping pile of roots, rocks, branches, mud. The topsoil had been peeled to bedrock in places, and the tang of ammonia hung in the air.

Mundeen whistled. The rest of us, standing silently, shared his awe. If the plane had made its run on our side of the saddle, some of us would have been hurt, maybe worse.

Cable swore at the pilot, shaking us out of it. He divided us into two man teams and spread us the length of the line. He said to drop back into the rocks if we got in trouble. Smoke was already rolling through the saddle, the fire not far behind.

I was paired with Cavenaugh, anchoring one end of the saddle. We started picking up spots ahead of the main fire front as embers carried across our line. We handled the early ones without much trouble, grinding out the sparks and small coals. Dense smoke funnelled through the saddle, stinging us with its acrid mix of burning bitterbrush and creosote. We crouched at intervals near the ground to get into clearer air. The worst spotting came as the fire reached our line. The embers kindled some of the brush and we were pressed to keep up. Cavenaugh grubbed up loose mounds of dirt with his pulaski, and I beat down the flames with loads of it.

We had our end pretty well tied up when a gust of flame bent over the crest and caught the brush near the middle of the saddle. Cavenaugh stayed to watch our sector and I went down the line to help out. The spot was spreading rapidly, its bitter smoke almost paralyzing. I threw a few ineffectual loads of dirt and dropped to the ground to clear my lungs and eyes. Near me, Orem was spread on the ground, coughing hard, gagging, tears steaming from his eyes. Cominsky hacked away with his pulaski, knelt for a few breaths, swung away again. Cavenaugh joined him, but the three of us made small headway. A flare-up drove us back, costing us the little line we had managed to build. Our fire spawned more spot fires, and we backed off further as the flames infected more brush.

"We can't hold her," said Cavenaugh, verifying what we all knew by now. "We can't hold the bitch."

"Where the hell is everybody else?"

"They're having trouble at the other end," said Cominsky. "Cable said to hang on till he gets here."

"Hang the hell on to what?" said Cavenaugh.

Orem was puking from the smoke. A thin bile dripped from his mouth after each spasm. We dragged him back as the fire came on. My eyes blurred with soot and tears as I slung dirt against the flames. We had doused our bandanas with water and knotted them across our faces, but the heat dried them quickly and the smoke filtered through potently, finding the last remote crevice in my lungs. The fire moved laterally on the hill, its downslope progress slowed in backing away from itself, unable to pre-heat the brush beneath it. Still, without a line under it, the fire would soon kick burning chunks down the ridge and the whole drainage would be lost. As we backed away, I tried to keep track of a boulder-strewn area near the bluff. When we pulled out, it would be our safest spot.

Erratic winds through the saddle combined with the fire's own currents to assemble small fire whirls of sparks and dust. One of the larger whirls sucked the smoke away from us and I saw Cable, Jimmy beside him, no more than two hundred feet away. They had turned the far corner of the spot fire and were well across the bottom. They reaped the brush in tandem, their hooks rising and falling like pistons. Behind them, Mundeen threw their brush while some of the rest of the crew dug a trench line. Cable's arm gave his hooking a jerky, uneven motion compared with Jimmy's fluid swing. I had been impressed with their work before, but I had never seen anything like this. The wreckage of brush in their wake was awesome.

Cominsky helped Orem back out of the smoke; Cavenaugh and I circled across to help with the line. As we came up, I could see Cable's eyes, red and squinted in his triumphant face. The words came out, one at a time, to the rhythm of his hook.

"Not this time—whore, bitch, mother. Not this time."

Jimmy's attention seemed fixed somewhere ahead, as though he were willing the line complete. The accuracy of his swing appeared to take place without his direct concentration.

I had just started to knock some of the heat out of the fire for them when Cable's vise wrenched loose from its fitting. The force of the swing dug the metal into the stub of his arm. Cable let out a sharp animal sound of pain, then swore. There was no way to patch the apparatus back together. Mundeen stepped in beside Jimmy, but the wind had shifted; the smoke and heat now formed a searing wall that Mike couldn't stand up to. Jimmy went on, his only concession a cocking of his head away from the heat. Cable yelled for more shovels and dropped in behind Jimmy, throwing the cut brush with his good arm. Moya and Pitkin came up the line and the three of us did what we could, launching cargos of dirt against the flames.

Cable jerked out his radio and called the spotter plane.

"Two Alpha Tango, this is Dalton."

"This is Two Alpha Tango, go ahead."

"Yeah, Carson, we've got a cooker down here in the saddle. Can you break loose a 17 and give us a load?"

The radio spit some static.

"I didn't copy that." Cable adjusted the squelch on his set.

"Ten-six, Bob. I'm going ten-ninety-nine to airnet."

The spotter came back on channel a few minutes later.

"That's a negative on your request. I can't get anything to you for an hour. I have you in sight. Suggest that you back off until we can get some retardant on it."

"We can handle it," said Cable.

"Ten-four. Two Alpha Tango clear."

"Dalton."

Cable looked around.

"You heard the man; it's us or nothing."

Moya curled back his lip, speaking through his teeth. "Fuck the air force. We got what we need."

Cominsky came up through the smoke and said that the rest of the line was holding. Cable grabbed the socket of his fitting and wrenched it around on his arm.

"Let's do it."

We poured ourselves into it, matching finesse and staying power against the relentless burning. Time blurred and stuck in some expanded present, cut off from past and future. Then it was done. We came out into clear air and tied the line in, back into our main line.

I slumped to the ground and looked around. Everyone's eyes were swollen and blood red. Smoke-crusted faces were clotted with tears, sweat, and snot. Jimmy had a long, ugly welt of a blister on his neck, and Cable had dried blood on his metal arm where its sleeve had eaten into his flesh. The crew gathered until we were all there.

"Nice work," said Cable softly, his voice grainy from the smoke. "You earned every inch of that line." He coughed the catch out of his voice.

"You can live the rest of your lives and never see a man do what Jimmy did here today." Cable turned to him. "*Hermano*, for this one you should cut a gold notch in your hook."

Jimmy closed his eyes slowly, then opened them. "*Hermano*, I never can make another thing like it again."

To the west, a great pillar of smoke rose from another flank of the fire. North, the fire had passed over a main ridge. The ridge rode the skyline like a burned out battleship, scallops of flame still working here and there on the smoking hulk.

The spotter came back on the radio, asking if we still needed the airdrop.

"Negative," said Cable, "it's all wrapped up down here."

VIII

We waited into the night for a relief crew. North and west from the saddle, we watched the running fire squalls on distant ridges; above them, the smoke-lit sky had a sick, deathly glow. We built a warming fire and clustered around it. At that elevation, night temperatures slide into the forties, even in August.

We were mostly quiet, indrawn. Cable talked to fire camp on the radio. The scheduled relief crew wouldn't be up till morning. A few of the crew still coughed from the smoke; many of us kept washing our eyes with water, trying to clean out the sooty grit.

"That's about as bad as I've seen it," said Cavenaugh. "That was one nasty bunch of smoke."

"About as bad?" said Jarvis. "If it got any worse, I'd have to chisel this shit out of my eyes."

"It gets worse," said Cavenaugh. "Maybe not so much worse, but longer. How long were we in it—an hour and a half, maybe two?"

"Something like that."

"I've been on slash burns in Oregon where you had to hang in the smoke four or five hours. When you burn a clear-cut unit up there, you do it slow so it doesn't get away from you. With all the rotten slash in the unit, you end up with a ton of smoke. Since you started the fire, you've got to hang in there and make sure it stays in the unit. It gets so bad I've seen guys go squirrely after while, or just get real slow. Somebody said it was all the carbon monoxide. Sometimes even guys who don't smoke are coughing up crud two or three days afterwards. It gets to your eyes too. I'll bet tomorrow everything's out of focus, and bright light's gonna feel like somebody was working on you with a needle. A friend of mine went to a doctor about it once and he said it was because all that junk scratches your corona or something like that. It goes away after a day or two by itself, as long as you didn't catch a hot one that blistered your eyeball. Then you got trouble."

"I wonder if you ever get used to the smoke?" Stinson was working on his eyes with a wet bandana. "I mean, maybe it doesn't bother you so much once you get used to it."

"Sure," said Mundeen, "it's just like freezing to death. After you've done it once, there's nothing to it."

We crowded the warming fire—sleeping, waking up shaking with cold, sleeping again. Finally, the fire went out, and we hugged ourselves, snuggled into the dirt, inches from each other but never—not even in cold and exhaustion and sleep—touching. The worst of it was just before sunrise, at the first cornice of gray light to the east. You connect light with warmth; when it doesn't come, the cold feels more potent.

I was sitting up, smoking, when the idea came to me. Most of the crew was awake, except for Kruger, Stonecrofter, and Cominsky. Kruger was stretched out on his back, arms behind his head. I tried out my plan on Stinson, and he agreed. I lit another cigarette and Stinson slipped over to Kruger, knotting his bootlaces together. I drew on the cigarette until it had a good coal, and looked over at Mundeen who gave me thumbs up. I laid the cigarette on Kruger's crotch. We all watched in anticipation as smoke curled up and a brown scorch spread on Kruger's jeans. He shifted a little, but the cigarette stayed in place.

Kruger came awake with a howl, grabbing frantically at his crotch and leaping up. He went sprawling as the laces locked his feet, and rolled in the dirt, tearing at his belt, trying to get his pants down, still bellowing.

The crew whooped, cheered, and laughed. Even Jimmy joined in, his body shaking with shrill giggles.

"I been bit! Something fucking stung me!" Kruger yanked down his shorts. A red blister had begun to rise on his cock. The laughter began to register as he lay there, dabbing spit on the blister with his finger. He looked down at his knotted boots, then noticed the smoldering cigarette.

"You fuckers did it. Somebody's gonna be hurting for this. Who did it?" Kruger began yanking at his laces. "Whatever prick did it is gonna wish he hadn't."

"I only see one prick around here," said Moya innocently.

Kruger glared at him. "Mike, which one of them did it?"

"It was a team effort," said Mundeen. "Let it go; it ain't gonna kill you."

"Here." Cable pitched a tube of burn ointment from the first aid belt. Kruger freed his laces, then put on some of the salve. He walked over and picked up the cigarette. I was glad I'd thought to tear off the end with the filter and label. He hurled the cigarette into the burn.

"When I find out, there's gonna be blood." The steam had gone out of him and he said it sulkily.

"You're so bad," said Moya, "I bet you pick your nose both holes at the same time."

"OK," said Cable.

The relief crew climbed into sight on the ridge around seven-thirty. They came up slowly, leaning on their tools, stragglers strewn hundreds of yards behind the leaders.

"Here comes the cavalry," said Mundeen. "The tokay troopers."

The crew, almost fifty men, was entirely Mexican, many of them on the fat side of forty. Some of the younger crewmen had flames and eagles painted on their hard hats. Cable talked with their crew boss and the Forest Service liaison officer while the crew gradually accumulated in the saddle. One of them shouted to Moya in Spanish and he went over and talked for a while. As we lined out in cutting order to start down the ridge, Jarvis asked Moya what they'd been talking about.

"Oh," said Moya, "they just wanted to know how I could stand working with all this white paint."

"What did you say?"

Moya grinned wickedly. "I told him gringos are people too; you just got to make allowances. They got a great sense of smell. Where would the world be without them?"

As we worked our way toward fire camp, Cominsky and Mundeen began speculating on breakfast.

"I hope it's not the same outfit we got up here on the Adobe Fire."

"You mean the fire Johnny Cash started?"

"Yeah," said Mundeen. "What was their name—Grubsteak, Grubworm?"

"I remember," said Cominsky, "the one that served ham all the time."

"That's them. Hogburger Catering. Grease and sowshit with pig pie for dessert. I can't even look at a piece of bacon ever since without puking. I wonder if they ever arrested him for that."

"My wife read in T. V. Guide where they're trying to make him pay what it cost to put it out, but some Indian tribe says it's really their land and they don't care if he burned up some of it."

"Maybe they could let him play a benefit concert for hotshot crews, you know, like he does in prisons. Then Snead wouldn't have to go to jail to hear him."

The catering service turned out to be an outfit called Cielo.

"We're in business," said Moya. "These boys speak the right language. They'll talk to your stomach like a lover."

Moya was right. Breakfast was hot, ample, and good. After eating, we gathered in a roped-off sleeping area. There were no cots, but Cable had gotten some paper sleeping bags from supply.

I managed to sleep in snatches. The heat, dust, and racket of fire camp made long stretches of sleep impossible. Half-awake, from ground level, the scene was a kinetic assembly of purpose, sliding in and out of the surreal.

The Forest had mobilized for a campaign fire. More crews rolled in all day and helicopters ferried them out to the lines. Hotshot crews from the Cleveland and San Bernardino National Forests, Mexican contract crews, pickup crews from Bakersfield and Fresno, trustees from the state prison and county crews from juvenile detention camps—the fire camp clogged with men and a glut of machinery: Bell, Hiller, and quick, odd-looking Alouette helicopters, platoons of D-8 cats and an armada of tankers, diesel generators, loudspeakers, buses, semis, pickups, fuel trucks, tool grinders, banks of stoves and refrigeration equipment. All this moved or worked among the congestion of tents, tarps, trailers, benches and trestle tables, portable toilets, wash troughs, garbage cans, crates, barrels, boxes, and tanks. A congregations of odors converged with the heat and dust: the smells of smoke, gas, diesel, outhouses, sweat, food, and garbage coming, going, mingling. A maze of ropes, hung with flagging and cardboard signs, set aside areas for eating, sleeping, maintenance, supply, and for the fire boss and his support staff: plans chief, camp boss, meteorologist, safety officer, public information, tanker boss, tractor manager, air attack boss, line boss, liaison, finance, and timekeeping. The whole welter of men and gear, slowly coming into focus on the fire.

We went back on the line late in the afternoon. Cable had gotten his arm re-rigged so he could work with it. He seldom made reference to it, but when he came back with it fixed he said he was lucky he didn't need a doctor—just a good welder and mechanic. Doctors, he said, tried to fine-tune the apparatus as though it were a skittery foreign sports car when all it needed was soldering and a shot of grease.

Cable filled us in while we waited at the heliport for a ride. The fire was three thousand acres and moving strongly on its northwest front. Much of the terrain it was now burning in was too steep for cats and inaccessible to tankers. It was going to be a hand line show.

I'd hoped for a ride in an Alouette, but when my turn came up Cominsky and I were strapped into a Bell G-3B, a diminutive threeseater without doors. In the air, the Bell felt like an intricate, fragile toy, vulnerable to the slightest whim of wind. The control panel looked complicated enough for a B-52. I sat on the outside, next to where the door should have been. Looking down over my shoulder, I could feel my stomach bottom out as we cleared a ridge at a hundred feet and the canyon fell away, suddenly a thousand feet below the skids. Cominsky looked rigidly ahead. When I glanced over at him, his eyes were closed. The helicopter banked in and eased down on a helispot carved out on a ridgeline. The prop wash drove violent clouds of dust into the brush as the pilot held the engine at full power. We scrambled away from the ship and it lifted off, dropping backwards down the slope, gathering speed, then pivoting gymnastically and climbing away.

"Jesus," said Cominsky, "if he'd done that coming in I'd have flat croaked."

"How could you tell one way or the other with your eyes closed?"

"I could tell. All I'd have to do is check my shorts for skid marks."

We cut line all night, tying in our sector to a line cut by the Del Rosa Hotshots from the San Bernardino. They had cut good line—wide, clean, well-trenched. We had cut better line, and the intersection was as distinct as crossing a border on a highway.

Helicopters carried us back to fire camp. Cable checked in with our division boss while we lined up for breakfast. We had finished eating and were back in our sleeping area before he returned. His stiff walk and rigid face meant something was wrong. He took Moya aside and they talked. After a while, they went off toward the overhead area. Cable came back alone. We had no idea what was on its way—only that it was something we weren't going to like. None of us could have been prepared for how remote our uneasiness was from the facts that were to come.

"There's something I want you to hear from me before you start hearing it from assholes that don't know what they're talking about. What it comes to is this: Calendar and Perez started this fire and they're both dead."

Nobody said anything. Fire camp wheeled on around us as we sat there, absorbing it, waiting for Cable to say the rest. My stomach felt like it had in the helicopter.

"I just talked to the arson man from the regional office and the FBI. There was another guy in on it, some college buddy of Calendar's. They got the story from him. Calendar set it all up. He was mixed up with one of those Communist outfits that want to take over America. He figured setting fires would help them do that. That's why he signed on with Dalton, to find out the best way to set fires. I don't know how Perez got into it. So they set three fires, except on the last one this other guy busted his ankle coming out. Calendar wanted to leave him there and Perez wouldn't. They got into it and Calendar shot him in the stomach. Perez died for a long time. There was nothing the other guy could do. Calendar was coming down when he missed a curve up Sixes Canyon. The wreck started a fire and a tanker crew found his body in the car."

A helicopter wound its engine and lifted off the pad. It banked over fire camp like a great bird of prey.

"That's the whole thing; that's everything they told me. Except they want to talk to anybody that knows anything else about it."

"Jesus," said Mundeen softly. "Jesus mothering Christ."

"We'll be going back on the line tonight," said Cable. "The only thing we can do is work our way out of it."

Nobody talked at first. We sat there into the afternoon, drenched in heat and dust, each of us trying to accommodate hard and final facts. When Moya came back, I went over to him. "I'm sorry," I said.

"It's none of your business."

We cut line that night and again the next. We began to talk about it a little, trying to fill or bridge the cavity that had opened in our sense of how the world worked. It felt partly like a death in the family. More, though, it seemed a profound and ugly contamination, a betrayal of the bedrock bond of men whose work demanded they be able to count on each other absolutely. However we twisted it, our response was inconsequential: it had happened, and it was immutable. Angry with our gingerly arrangement of explanations, Mundeen set himself against them, straightforward and conclusive.

"Look. Everybody knows Calendar had some screwy ideas. He was flipped out before he ever showed up at Dalton. He knew what he was doing, and it doesn't have anything to do with the rest of us. There's nothing we could have done. Perez was a jerk to get sucked in, but he's a big boy. Nobody twisted his dick. He knew what he was buying into."

I reran the season in my head, playing it back for hints I should have picked up, deductions I might have made. I didn't have the guts to ask what Perez had been shot with. I would have to work out how to live with myself not knowing that. The Luger would make no difference now to anyone but me.

By the fifth night on the line, grinding fatigue had deadened our capacity to think about it. Marathon runners have a name for what happens at that point in a race, somewhere around twenty miles, when your body is finally broken down beyond replenishment and must cannibalize itself to keep going. They call it hitting the wall. Beyond the wall on campaign fires, you run on courage, instinct, and the knowledge that if you break, the rest of the crew pays for it in picking up your slack.

Most of us had hit that wall by our fifth shift. The bonesunk exhaustion was studded with specific pain: raw blisters, sprains, raspy lungs, eyes gritty from smoke, cramped muscles and bowels. No matter how much fresh fruit I ate, no matter how much juice and water I poured down in fire camp, sweat sucked the moisture from me on the line, cinching my intestines into a solid knot. Smoke-stained and dirt-clotted, we went without enough sleep, never enough sleep; the work going on, getting done. Mundeen had another term for it, brought with him from football. He called it playing hurt.

By our fifth shift, the fire had been pinched down into an irregular front, burning in broken, spidery, gully country. There were still flare-ups as the fire made spastic runs up the network of ravines, but now most of the firefighting forces could be concentrated in one area. Cable said the fire boss thought we'd have a line around the whole thing by morning.

Cutting line in that kind of country was frustrating. The erratic burning and terrain left long peninsulas of unburned brush, crooked inlets of fire. We wove our line around the living brush, following the edge of the burn. Often, we cut hundreds of feet to gain thirty feet of straight line. We worked automatically, frugally. I learned early that angry attack on unyielding roots or brush cost me more than I could afford. The trick was to stay with it in small increments.

We had gotten through most of the shift when a small canyon went off. Just before it caught, we had seen a string of headlamps ahead and knew that we were close to tying our line in. The smoke rolled over us, at least as dense and bitter as it had been that afternoon in the saddle. We were working near the rim of the canyon, and had to chase down a few spot fires behind our line. I was working on one with Snead and Jarvis when Pitkin passed word up that he needed a hook at the end of the line. Cable sent Speyer back to help out.

A few feet from me, Jarvis and Snead glowed like phantoms in my headlamp beam. There were few spots and little heat, but the smoke had us on the ropes this time. We could only cover up and try to hold on until the canyon burned itself out. We had managed to extinguish our spot when Speyer came back past in a crouching run. Moments later, Cable pulled us back down the line to find Pitkin.

We stumbled through the brush and smoke, coughing, shouting, pumping our last reserves of adrenalin. We must have searched for twenty minutes in the smoke, then ten more as the fire laid down all at once and the air cleared. I wasn't far from Cavenaugh when he found Pitkin. He was well down in the canyon, two hundred feet or more from our line. Dick was on his stomach, his headlamp shining feebly in the dirt. He wasn't breathing.

Cable rolled him on his back and felt for a pulse. He brought the heel of his hand down hard on Dick's ribs, then bent and began forcing breath into his mouth; rocked back, pumping his rib cage, bent again to charge his lungs. Cable worked on him for a long time. He leaned back finally; reached down absently and flicked off Dick's headlamp.

After a while, Cable called fire camp. A helicopter would be in at first light to pick up the body.

Cominsky took off his fire shirt and laid it over Dick's face. We sat together near the body.

A wave of whoops and cheers rolled down the canyon. The crew we had seen had tied into our line.

Cable asked Speyer what had happened. Speyer spoke thoughtfully, but without hesitation.

"When I first got back, he seemed disoriented and I asked if he was all right. He shouted something garbled, then he wobbled and went down. When I got to him, he seemed to be unconscious and was having trouble breathing. I went down on him and started to give him mouth-to-mouth resuscitation. He began thrashing like a drowning man. He knocked me off-balance and ran downhill through the brush. I followed him by sound, but when the sound stopped I knew I could never find him in the smoke. That's when I came back."

The news about Calendar and Perez had shaken us badly; Dick's death left us stunned, broken. Men from other crews came up in fire camp, sympathetic, asking clumsy questions. Cable spent a long time with the fire overhead. Sometime during the day, the fire was declared contained. When they were finished with Cable, we started on the long road back to Dalton.

On the way back, I tried to find a passage that might lead between the disorder of causes, the closure of consequence—some vantage point where the continuity would come clear. I kept circling back to Kelly and her tarot. I hadn't connected Perez's and Calendar's deaths to her prediction. Their separation from the crew seemed to exempt them. I wasn't so sure that was the case anymore, but it hardly mattered. Dick's death stood as confirmation of Kelly's warning. To acknowledge that was like going to sleep in one room and waking up in another. I struggled with the fearful indisputability of it, the long implications of believing it to be true.

That night, Cable called us together in the mess hall. It was a mute gathering. Most of us hadn't showered or changed clothes. The smell of stale sweat and smoke clung in the air. Cable looked around at us.

"I want to say some things before all this starts festering up. I've been here before. I know how that goes." Cable looked like he hadn't closed his eyes in a week.

"I've said all there is to about Perez and Calendar. That's finished unless somebody's got something they want to say."

Nobody did.

"About Pitkin; that was my fault all the way. I'm paid to stop fires and keep you guys in one piece. Any time I can't do that, I'm not doing my job. The overhead isn't going to see it that way. They already told me there was nothing I did wrong, nothing I could have done. I don't buy that. I knew the canyon was ready to go, but I didn't figure on that much smoke. I should have sent more men back with Speyer to help out. That's two more mistakes than a fire's going to give you—two mistakes I have to live with. They said it was all some kind of fluke. If I can't handle what comes up, I got no business running a crew."

It was clear that Cable believed what he was saying. I didn't, and I don't think anyone else did either.

"Some of you know a lot about fire, and the rest of you are learning. If you make mistakes, maybe we lose a line. If I make a mistake, we're playing for the whole pot. Maybe tomorrow we'll roll again and we're gonna be out there and you're gonna have to take my word for what we're doing. And I can tell you right now, I'll be damned if I'm gonna back off like some gun-shy lieutenant. We're gonna go after it as hard as we ever did. I want you to think about that right now. This isn't the Army. Anybody who doesn't want to do that has every right to walk. Every right. It's nothing I'd hold against a man. You've got to believe in the man up front. You shouldn't be here otherwise. I don't want you here otherwise."

The power and urgency of Cable's voice cracked like a whip across our paralysis. It was Moya who spoke for us.

"You don't see nobody getting up. You don't hear nobody blaming you either. You want to blame yourself, you blame yourself. If I'm gonna put my ass on the line, I know who I want out there telling me when to sit and when to shit."

"That's the size of it," said Mundeen. "That's how it looks from here."

"OK," said Cable, an uncomfortable hitch in his voice. "OK." I just want anyone who feels different to remember what I said."

He waved us out. "Go get yourselves cleaned up. Christ, you smell like you've been fighting fire or something."

Cable never talked about any of the three of them again after the next day. He told us that the coroner's preliminary report indicated that Pitkin had died from smoke inhalation, possibly aggravated by some kind of asthmatic or allergic reaction to the particular composition of the smoke. Dick's funeral was scheduled for the following day. Anyone who wanted to take leave without pay could go.

The service was held in a funeral home I had seen advertised on late night television. The building blended into its block on a heavily travelled street. It was bracketed by a bowling alley and a discount appliance store. I was the only member of the crew who showed up. Cable was there, along with a middle-aged couple and their daughter. In his dark suit and skinny tie, Cable looked like a gambler with a long string of losses. The woman was Pitkin's aunt.

The service was brief. The woman's husband hiccupped mildly and kept looking at his watch. The funeral director, or whoever it was that spoke, looked sleepy. He had to step behind the curtains to shut off the recorded organ music when it began to replay after he'd started speaking.

Cable left as soon as it was over, pausing to say something to the couple. Outside, I went up to them and said something awkward. The little girl was holding her mother's hand.

"Maybe it's all for the best," the woman said. "He never had much of a life. I don't expect he would have even if this hadn't of happened."

"I don't want Dick to be dead," said the girl.

The woman looked down. "God knows what's best, Sissy. God knows what He wants to happen."

"Will God make somebody come play with me then?"

The man honked from the curb.

"Thank you for coming. I know how much Dick's friends at work meant to him." As they walked to the car, Sissy turned around and waved at me. I raised my hand in return.

I thought about going to the Midway to see if Cable was there. Instead, I drove, stopped at some tavern, drove some more, and finally called Kelly. I called off and on for most of the afternoon.

Karen finally answered. I asked for Kelly.

"The only reason I don't hang up is because I've got something to tell you first. Kelly's not here and I'm not going to say where she is. She just broke down when she heard about it; I mean she broke down so bad I had to take her to a doctor. How do you like that, Mr. Know-Everything, Mr. Hotshot? All because you wouldn't listen to her. I'm not going to let this wreck her whole life, but it could do that very, very easily. She never wants to see you again, and I'll make sure she doesn't. I hope you get what you deserve. Asshole." She banged the phone down.

I came out of the phone booth, my shirt stuck to my back from sweating out the afternoon's beer. My body felt like a brittle barrier against an emptiness that had come into the world. Only that vulnerable husk of flesh contained my own losses, preserved them from dissolution into that outer, mindless waste.

I wanted to break down sobbing or to rage; to be comforted and absolved. But the mind grinds on, addicted to its familiar furrows. Whatever my future, it would be always in complicity with this past. Clamped by that compact, my only allegiance could be to understanding, to deciphering whatever terms the past could exact from the rest of my life.

I felt a spreading infection of guilt for Kelly's breakdown, even if

Karen might have exaggerated it. Logically, it should have been hard to accept responsibility. Who could be held accountable for not believing in clanking claims for the supernatural until a flying saucer or ghost conclusively, personally presented itself? Besides, firefighting was chancy work. That Kelly's prediction came true might be nothing more than coincidence—bitter and lethal, but nothing more than random chance.

As Speyer had said, it takes a personality tilted toward neurosis to believe in the occult. It shouldn't have been a surprise that Kelly would warp into certifiable craziness under the pressure of foretelling a death. Maybe she had even come to confuse prediction with cause.

However it worked, and whatever it was, Kelly's pathology or cold-blooded truth, I told myself that what I had said and done had caused nothing—what I might have done or said could not have made any difference. I am willing to lie in context, for the overriding good of myself or for someone who needs the lie more than I need the truth. To have told Kelly I believed in her tarot, even to have accepted her ultimatum about quitting, would have been a lie that could not have changed Dick's death. If Kelly really could read the future, she would have to bear the consequences. If she could not, maybe this would bring her out the other side to a balanced skepticism of a fantastic, separate reality. Either way, I could not work out a grammar of blame with myself as the object. But beyond these skimpy perimeters of rationality, there where most of my life went on, I was guttered with guilt.

Calendar and Perez presented another moral tangle. Why hadn't I told Cable about the pistol? Why hadn't I gotten rid of it myself? Was Perez dead because of that? If the gun was, in fact, the one Calendar used, wouldn't he have gotten another just as easily? My responsibility felt both more oblique and more direct than for Kelly. My place in what happened was that of a tooth in a gear of the blind machinery of events. Even if I hadn't occupied that slot, I could never know whether the sequence might have come to a different end.

I drove automatically back to Dalton. Walking into the barracks, my eyes sought out the three empty bunks. They stood like coffins through the rest of the season. The deaths altered the character of the crew. After the Bouquet Fire, there was little of the complex give and get that creates a crew as a unit, maintains it as an organism. Sealed up in the mountains, we isolated ourselves from each other.

Moya drove in late that night. I hadn't been able to sleep and had finally gone outside. He got out of his car and sat with me on the mess hall steps. Moya had gone to Requiem Mass for Perez. Now he was thick with tequila, still drinking from a quart bottle. I shared the last of it with him. We passed the bottle, not saying anything, drinking in the dark against our casualties.

"I wish Calendar was alive. Busted up bad, but alive." Moya's voice sounded lethally sober.

"Why?"

"We was blood, Jorge and me. When Calendar got out of the hospital, I'd be there. I'd do it so he'd die piece by piece."

"Were you and George related?"

"Cousins."

"What about the other guy with them?"

"It wouldn't be the same. I met him a couple time. He's just a jerk; he didn't know how far in he was gonna get. Just like Jorge. The poor, dumb, stupid prick. He never could look out for himself. Maybe Calendar has a brother. You think he has a brother?"

"I don't know. Did Calendar try to suck you in?"

"Sure," said Moya. "Me and Snead both."

"Why didn't you?" I didn't really care what I asked. I just wanted someone else's words to override the monologue in my head.

"I ain't no altar boy, but setting fires is chickenshit. And it don't have nothing to do with Chicanos being fucked over. You want to make a difference about being fucked over, you go after what's fucking you. Running around like a little kid with matches is chickenshit and it don't make any difference."

"Snead too?"

"He'd done it if Calendar wasn't such an asshole. Snead, he'd burned up the whole fucking country if Calendar had any style at all."

Moya passed the quart and I took a throat-searing swallow. I rolled the bottle between my palms.

"Maybe Calendar has a brother. Assholes have brothers just like anybody else. You think Calendar has a brother?"

"I don't know." I took another drink. The bottle was almost empty.

"Did the FBI lean on you?"

"Sure, they tried to. That's one edge you get being a greaser. Somebody tries to come down on you, you know how to slide out from under."

"What are you going to do now?"

"Stick around," said Moya. "I'm gonna stick around. When Calendar's brother shows up, I'm gonna be here."

I passed the tequila and Moya finished it.

"I never been shot in the guts," said Moya. "Have you?"

"No."

"You figure it hurts as bad as you think?"

"Yeah," I said. "I figure it would."

"The poor, dumb, stupid prick. He never could look out for himself. And now he's got himself snuffed." Moya giggled. "I'll bet it pissed him off. I'll bet it pissed him off that I was too smart to be there." He stopped giggling. "We was blood. He needed me."

Suddenly, I didn't want to say any more, hear any more. I walked away, leaving Moya there with the new bottle he'd pulled out of his shirt.

In the morning, we found Moya passed out near his car and carried him to his bunk. There wasn't much talk at breakfast. Stonecrofter's and Stinson's parents had tried to get them to quit. Both had refused. As we walked out to the obstacle course, I heard Cominsky talking to Cavenaugh.

"I been thinking, maybe it's like the wife says. Like actors and plane crashes. They always happen three at a time."

I talked with Speyer often in the next days. We went out after supper, walking up the ridge, the crests of the Santa Sangres blood-hooded by the last of the sun. Dark came earlier as the season sloped toward fall.

I poured myself out to Speyer—my doubts, my guilt, my confusion. Trying to pry some discovery out of language, I thrashed in a thicket of words. He listened to my disarray, and when he spoke the wash of his voice was stroking, healing; the sense of his words arranged islands of clarity.

He insisted I shouldn't feel responsible for the consequences of actions I did not intend, acts that were contaminated by disordered or deliberate motives of others. He pointed out the imperfect basis upon which we make decisions about our conduct, and that moral accountability can only derive from moral intent. If we have been misled, or even naive in forming our judgments, we should only regret our limited perspective, not find ourselves corrupt. That I blamed myself as an instrument in Perez's death and Kelly's breakdown was, in fact, validation of my human concern, not my complicity.

"You might find it helpful to look at it with respect to my own circumstance." We had been talking about my feeling that if I had only read Calendar right, I could have guessed his purpose and somehow deflected him.

"I spent a lot of time with Larry, certainly more than you, perhaps as much as anyone here. We talked a great deal about social and political systems. I found him angry, certainly, and intense, but intellectually bound—a man of theories, not a man of the streets. Most people who work for the Forest Service fantasize about setting fires. It's the attraction of opposite principles—the preacher and the whore; the itch to use a proscribed skill. And it is our unacknowledged lust for apocalypse. Of any of us, I had the best opportunity to judge his capacity for acting out his romance of revolution. I just didn't think it was a real possibility."

"I have found myself to be perceptive, not perfect. I regret those imperfections, but I refuse to blame myself for them. It seems to me that your limited access to Larry gives you even less reason for guilt."

Speyer had already enabled me to discard my sense of responsibility for the pistol, and had helped greatly with my tangle about Kelly. He even thought she might grow to appreciate how little I had to do with the destructive path she had set for herself. To have taken her seriously could only have urged her that much further into the wilderness.

Speyer looked on the fulfillment of her prediction as a tragic coincidence. "Of course, there's always the chance that it involved more than random correspondence. If that were the case, it represented a unique collision of the ordinary and the unnameable that likely will never take place for her again. I don't discount such events; it would be foolish to deny what cannot by its nature be verified. But coincidence is by far more probable. I would think her greatest stress will come when she recognizes that predictions are profoundly connected to desires. Why she should hope for such an outcome for Dalton is a psychological knot only a professional could unravel. Certainly, it's a knot that was woven long before she met you."

We talked a little about Pitkin. I kept my resolve not to tell Speyer about Dick's dream of him. It seemed a cruel fact for a man who had taken some chances trying to save Dick's life. We agreed that Dick must have been completely disoriented when he broke away from Speyer and fled into the burn. Had he stayed near the line, where our initial search was concentrated, he would have been found sooner, perhaps saved. Speyer spoke of his puzzlement at Dick's violent reaction to him.

"He was like a drowning man, or a madman in an asylum. It served no purpose to tell anyone, but I was not thrown off-balance. He simply overpowered me. His strength was astonishing. He acted as if I were trying to harm him. Even in his state, I can't imagine how he came to that unless it was somehow connected to the time I found him going through my things in the barracks. I wasn't especially harsh with him about it, but he was clearly terrified when I caught him. Other than that, we hardly had anything to do with each other. I suppose his derangement from the smoke could have swollen that incident into something more than it was."

Talking with Speyer, listening to him, brought me back into balance. Tangled in blame, my own attempts to justify my conduct had sounded like tinny rationalizations. From the perspective of Speyer's moral maturity, I learned to distinguish explanations from excuses; not to wallow in self-abusive guilt when straight thinking could penetrate the moral murk. Speyer's array of logic seemed a wonderfully engineered bridge, carrying me with elegance and precision across the abyss of garble and silence. I was relieved, and grateful.

"If I've been of some help, I'm gratified. Irrational guilt is paralytic; it is the great sickness of Western man. It has maimed us all. Any piece of ourselves we can win back from it brings us nearer our right and our glory: a free mind, capable of anything; the dignity of unfettered movement through this world."

A week or so after the funerals, we were hanging around the compound after lunch, waiting to go out on project work, when a car appeared on the switchbacks leading up to camp. The car came slowly up, hugging the center of the road. We watched it with some curiosity. Except for Forest Service personnel, the only visitors to Dalton were occasional stray tourists who had taken two or three wrong turns.

The black Oldsmobile stopped near the mess hall and a small, fat man in a suit climbed down. He walked gingerly around the car toward us, tiptoeing through the dust that puffed up at each step.

"Hi, fellas," he said. "Sure is a hot one." He pulled out a handkerchief, folded it, and patted the sweat from his domed forehead.

"I'm looking for your manager."

Kruger nodded his head. "Inside."

The man picked his way over to the steps. Before he went in, he flapped the dust off his shoes with another handkerchief.

"What do you make of that?" asked Stinson.

"Maybe it's a new recruit," I said.

"Recruit my ass," said Kruger. "He looks like somebody drumming up business for an undertaker. Maybe Uncle's gonna offer us a funeral plan."

"He looks like the guys that kept coming around when my business went broke," said Cominsky. "Any of you owe money, you better light out for the brush."

The man came out a few minutes later. Cable was with him.

"This is Mr. G. I. Jacobs," Cable said. "He has a piece of paper that says Pitkin owed him a lot of money. He says he'd like to see if any of Dick's stuff is worth anything. I told him the crew would take care of him. I said you wouldn't mind helping him out."

Cable went back into the mess hall. Mr. Jacobs stood uncertainly on the steps. No one said anything.

"Terrible thing, what happened to Dick; a real tragedy. Well, boys, shall we have a look-see. It's business, you understand, strictly business."

"How much did Dick owe you?" I asked.

"That's a confidential matter," said Mr. Jacobs. "I assure you it's all here on paper. It's a legal obligation."

"The man asked you how much," said Mundeen.

"Oh," said Mr. Jacobs, looking around, "a trifle under six hundred dollars. Naturally, I don't expect to recover the full amount. I'm sure you boys agree that a man has an obligation to repay his debts. Shall we have that look-see now?"

"Why don't you tell us why Dick owed you six hundred dollars?" I was so angry my voice was shaking.

"That's none of your affair. Look here, I'm a reasonable man. I'd hate to involve the authorities. There's no reason for it to come to that, though. I can see you boys are reasonable."

"How did you get into Pitkin for six hundred, you oily little prick?" Mundeen had moved between Mr. Jacobs and his car.

"See here, you have no right to—"

"How?" snarled Snead, leaning against the mess hall near the door.

"Well, if it makes any difference, we played golf. Miniature golf. We ran little wagers, you know, just to keep it interesting."

"Shit," said Stinson. "I played with Pitkin once. I could have beat him left-handed."

Mr. Jacobs began edging toward the mess hall door. "I can see you don't understand what's involved here. I'll just have your manager straighten this out."

Snead grabbed him as he started up the steps. Mr. Jacobs squeaked as Snead hauled him back by the collar of his suit.

"I think we understand what's involved, all right," said Mundeen, walking up. "There's nobody here don't understand shit from an asshole

133

when it's spread right in front of them."

"I'm a reasonable man, boys, a reasonable man. Why don't we just forget all about this. Just forget it, no hard feelings?"

His face was reddening from Snead's grip.

"You're in luck, Mr. Jacobs," said Mundeen. "We're all reasonable too. Instead of just beating the puke out of you, we're gonna be reasonable."

Mr. Jacobs was sweating hard.

"Take off your clothes. Turn loose of him, Dean. Mr. Jacobs is gonna take his clothes off." Snead released his grip on the collar. Mr. Jacob's eyes bobbed around our circle. He broke toward the mess hall door.

"Help," he bleated, "somebody help me."

We bounced him back into the center of our ring.

"Take them off," said Mundeen.

Mr. Jacobs came out of his clothes slowly. He stopped when he got down to his shoes and shorts.

"Everything," said Mundeen.

When Mr. Jacobs was naked, Mundeen told him to give us his car keys and the paper that Pitkin had signed. When he had them, Mike told Kruger to take the ignition key off the ring, lock all the clothes in the trunk, and pitch the key ring.

"Now," said Mundeen, "I'd recommend you get the fuck out of here before we run out of reasonableness." We parted our circle as Mr. Jacobs went in a gingerly waddle toward the car, folds of flesh billowing. He let out a yip when he slid in on the hot upholstery, and ground the starter a long time before the car started. Mr. Jacobs didn't look back as he barreled out of the compound.

Cable came out of the mess hall when he was gone.

"Did Mr. Jacobs get what he needed?"

"Yeah," said Mundeen, "he got everything he had coming."

Since the Bouquet Fire, Jimmy had faded. The time I spent in Speyer's company helped neuter Jimmy's obscure and ominous monologues. If Speyer was different from the rest of us, it was the difference of a man who was legible, lucid: sure enough of himself to be genuinely involved with others. Jimmy's perverse abstraction of Speyer could only be motivated by willful misunderstanding, perhaps tainted by an atavistic mind less and less in touch with the world. How much his seizures had to do with it hardly mattered anymore.

Still, his uncanny presence, his implacable distance, seeped into my landscape like a pocket of fog in the high country—dissolving, reforming just ahead as you approached. I had been able to clear away or discount much of his cryptic translation of things. What remained were fragments of words and uneasy images that unearthed themselves when my mind went slack in sleep or wakeful puttering.

We had not talked since that night in the barracks after the party, and I had directly avoided him after I saw him come unmoored in the mountains. Our only affinity now was our common work. I was unprepared when Jimmy appeared one evening after I had worked my way far up the ravine east of the station. For several nights, just before sunset, coyote calls had funneled down the canyon. I had never seen a coyote, and thought I might trace one down by his voice. As I neared the head of the ravine, the light was far enough gone that twice I thought I saw movement only to find blank brush when I turned to look. Jimmy appeared quite close to me, on my left, coming out of some manzanita that didn't seem tall enough to have masked his approach. A little rinse of alarm passed across my groin. Having witnessed the phantom combat and his fit, I understood that Jimmy could be dangerous.

"So, you have not seen enough yet in the brush."

The rinse iced over into fear. He had seen me, had come across my tracks, knew I was there that day at the circle.

"You think you will find coyote by looking for him?" Jimmy's voice had an amused tint to it that left me guarded but no longer afraid.

"I'd like to," I said.

Jimmy spread his hands in front of him.

"If it is so, you will. But I do not think it is so."

"Why not?" I was annoyed now that he'd found me, followed me.

"Maybe," he said, shrugging it away.

"It's too late to see anything now anyway."

"Maybe you are right. Maybe your best way is to look straight on for a thing."

Again, Jimmy had tilted the ground between us, striking off obliquely from what I had said. In my irritation, I held myself against asking what he meant. I had spent all season asking that; I was through with it.

"So, I will say it straight ahead to you that you have made a wrong seeing. You have heard the snake song and it has filled up your ears against all other singing. I will say to you straight on how I must say to a child that your brujo is a thing of death. I will say to you only because you can not see with your best eyes and it is so long already, so close to you."

His voice was high, rapid, old, the words clusters of Zuni and Spanish cased in English. Their cadence drew me in, against my monitor of disbelief, the rhythm of his speech holding me like gravity within his field of vision.

"How the colors around him change, like the water where our spirits go at last; how the colors around the brujo are bright with the life he sucks from the mouth of the child who knew him. Now you know and maybe you can make the right way. Already he draws my breath and I must make my own way. I can not make little piles of myself for you. I am not hands-empty of weapons, but I must gather the luck of all my person against what comes. I can not help you now. Now, you can not help me. Make yourself small and close to the earth—a chip of rock, a bead of air, the beetle's underside. Do not be looked for."

Jimmy reached out, placing both palms hard against my belly, and said something in Zuni. The tone of the words and the level pressure of his hands felt like a benediction. He turned away and was gone in the brush.

———

IX

"This is odd work for a grown man. When you get right down to it, what it comes to for him is going on, season after season, dragging a bunch of post-teenagers along behind him. Fire by fire, line by line, hooked on it, gutted by it, alone with it, really; Jimmy too far gone to keep him company anymore. He's an original, out there somewhere beyond us all. There's never been anyone for him to imitate, no models except for some old idea of himself. It's no surprise he's ended up maimed. It would be a surprise if he hadn't." Speyer made a mild, almost elegant gesture with his hand.

"Cable's not whole, and fighting every fire from here to the Mexican line won't make him whole, because what he's trying to extinguish is his underlife that covets chaos—that erotic undermusic of Götterdämmerung. Most of us manage to deny that side, or at least ignore it. Cable can't. Which for him means he must try to kill it. And he'll go on crippling himself because what he's attacking is himself transferred to fire. Every skirmish he wins invites the holocaust. Who knows how long it can go on?"

We were walking again, early evening, the air of September still stiff with heat. Tonight, though, there was a difference. Speyer had begun to talk about Cable unprompted, without splicing it onto a question of mine. And the pulse of his language was not regular. It moved with jittery urgency, a current of emotion flickering in and out of it. No longer conveying disinterested speculation and evenhandedness, his speaking carried the weight of conclusiveness, the raw vibration of power.

This surge of authority was an uncanny tattoo, an echo of Jimmy's convinced speaking. Not that the tone or rhythms were similar, certainly not the language itself. But the necessity that drove the voice was unmistakable. I couldn't guess what had swung Speyer out of his equilibrium. The shift was unsettling, exciting. I had learned much from him; now I would learn more. I hardly needed to provoke him with questions. It kept coming, poise and polish overridden in the flow. He no longer reminded me of a foreigner, more stiffly precise in the language than a native speaker. Cable was his hub that first night; later, it would be Jimmy, with others illuminated as he ricocheted among the crew.

The pace of our walks increased. By the end of the week, we were covering maybe five miles altogether, in serpentine up the ridge and back. Speyer was always a little ahead of me, moving erectly through the brush, efficient, without grace or clumsiness, pausing, using his hands sometimes for punctuation.

"Korea is Cable's own metaphor for extremity. It is the true source of him, of whatever he has done since. Maybe, at the beginning anyway, his justification. Cable has depth, all right, but he's not complex. His eyes, all the way down, say just one thing: 'I have been there—I have been to the end of the road and seen that it only ends.' It doesn't matter that Korea will turn out to be pocket change compared to what America's up to in Asia this time. The ambiguity of the jungle could never be Cable's kind of war. Ambiguity. I could have given him that once. It is the only serum for obsession, all that can infect such sterile purity."

A few times I stepped into the flow, feeling my way. Before, Speyer had responded directly to my questions. Now he seemed to absorb them, the questions not so much responded to as incorporated, vanishing beneath his moving surface.

"You think Cable is replaying Korea here? Trying to settle something he never got straightened out over there, in the war?"

"What do you suppose will happen when he roots out his last complexity, when his last impediment to this monomania has been driven into psychological exile? A man who becomes nothing but his focused will is beyond human boundaries. He has gone into country where he cannot survive."

I seldom noticed when we turned back, was not often aware even of walking.

"Still, still, I am always astonished by how far a man scaled to one thing can go. I said Cable was an original. He is not, of course. Strictly, there is only one of everything. Yet there are others. No one he has ever known. And at that, there aren't many who approach his scale, his singleness. Calendar might have turned out something like that. It would have taken years, of course. And the one chunk he bit off choked him before he could ever really get his teeth into it. But Cable, he will go on chewing fire and when his teeth are gone he will gag it down and when his bowels quit on him he will bloat and tear at himself and perish."

Earlier, as though by arrangement, we had separated as we approached camp from our walks. We didn't go out of our way to hide it, but neither did we put our companionship on display. Now we walked straight in together. I usually went to the mess hall for coffee. Speyer always went directly to the shower room. He seemed to prefer showering by himself; few of the crew were ever there that time of evening.

One of those evenings, Cominsky and Bailey were sitting together in the mess hall when I came in. Bailey stopped talking and scuttled away into his room off the kitchen as I poured some coffee. Bailey often scurried; it seemed to be his normal gait. I could hear one lock, then another click as Bailey sealed himself in for the night.

I sat down across from Carl.

"You'd think this was the Bailey National Bank or something. Jesus, if this place ever caught fire, he'd never get out of there." I was accustomed enough to the coffee by now that I could swallow it without squinting.

"He might as well be a bank. You got any idea how much money he makes?"

I shook my head.

"Well, for starters he's a wage grade four. I looked it up once. That's six dollars, thirty-seven cents an hour, not counting per diem and time and a half and such. I bet he makes more money in a season than Bob does."

"Jesus," I said, "imagine what they'd have to pay somebody who knew how to cook. We're in the wrong business."

"Naw, they couldn't pay me enough to be a cook." Cominsky leaned back and patted his stomach with both hands. The summer hadn't removed all traces of the roll I remembered from June. "Eating's more my line of work."

Carl chuckled and I realized, with a twinge, surprised, that I was going to miss him. Plain and honest as a plate of potatoes.

"Did Bailey always lock himself up like that?"

"Well, it seems to me the first couple of years he was here he only had two locks."

"You mean he's got more than two locks on that door?"

"Well, now, he might have reason to."

"Like what?"

"Oh, I don't suppose it'd do any harm." Cominsky leaned down the table and picked up a magazine from the floor. "I thought he dropped one. That's probably what happens to them."

"Let's see."

Cominsky slid the magazine across the table. "He thinks somebody's stealing these from him, you know, just to get his goat."

The magazine was titled *Prosthesis Review.* It was published, according to its cover, by the Sarasota College of Prosthetics.

"He's taking one of those correspondence courses and they send him the magazine free. I guess some of them came up missing, and he figures the crew got hold of them. So I guess to his way of thinking, he needed some more locks."

"Maybe he just ought to get himself a safe."

"He said something about that himself."

I poured myself some more coffee and Carl got another glass of milk from the dispenser. I was so wired from Speyer, the usually potent seepage of caffeine didn't seem to have any effect.

"You're going to be heading out one of those days, going back to college?"

"Yeah," I said, "another couple of weeks I guess."

"You know, nothing against college kids or anything, but I wish we didn't have to hire them, not so many, anyway. Seems like every year we go into Santa Ana season short because all you guys go back to school." Cominsky wiped a rim of milk off his lip.

"You ever get through a fall without the Santa Anas?"

"It'd be a real odd year. I mean, they're not always rooflifters, but they let you know they're around. Maybe you'll see for yourself, maybe by the end of the week even. I can feel it," Cominsky tapped his ear with a finger, "right here."

I shook my head. "What do you mean?"

"Well, it's the darnedest thing, but I got so I can tell the feeling right off after this many seasons. It doesn't amount to much at first. Then it starts to feel like somebody's blowing up a balloon inside my head, and pretty soon I can't hardly hear for it. Soon as it gets bad enough it just pops, and that's that."

I knew the Santa Anas fed on the pressure differential between a vast desert high and a marine low. I hadn't thought about how the high, as it built, could affect something besides the weather.

"The doctor said it was just the air pressure and the way my ears are put together. It makes lots of other folks go cattywampus too. My wife, it upsets her, you know, cycle. Otherwise she's so regular you could set your clock by her. I did it one month and you know, I wasn't off more than twenty minutes."

The fire weather advisories hadn't predicted any Santa Ana patterns developing, not even in the long-range forecast. I wondered how reliable Carl's earache was.

"I never been wrong yet, that I can recall. Well, maybe once, but I was coming down with a real bad cold. Besides, you can tell by the way Jimmy's acting. All that mumbling to himself and walking right past you. The first time I saw him like that—let's see, that must be seven years ago now—I figured he'd got into some booze and gone nutty like Indians do, just rattling around looser than a pocketful of change. I guess he's got more like that all the time, especially this year, but you see if he doesn't just disappear here one of these days. Next time he shows up, you can count on a Santa Ana breaking. And I can count on my ear feeling human again."

Carl rubbed the ear with the heal of his hand. "It doesn't help, but I can't seem to keep myself from doing it."

"What's it like? I mean, how bad does it get?"

"Oh, about like a bad toothache."

"No, I mean on the line. You must have been on a bunch of Santa Ana fires."

"Enough to last me the rest of my life. It's not that you're on the line so much; in fact, most of the time you're not on the line at all, at least not the way you're used to it. Those fires do pretty much anything they want to. You don't cut line on them. You just stay out of their way until they're good and ready to quit. Like my daddy used to say, let the big dog eat."

"Didn't you ever stop one?"

"Yeah, once. We stopped one once at Malibu. At the beach." Carl chuckled. "Bob said the ocean was the only line he ever saw that was better than Dalton's. Did I ever tell you I got on TV on that one? They didn't interview me or anything, but they got a shot of me and two other guys working a spot fire. The wife saw the program and she said you could tell it was me even if you weren't expecting it. I saw it on a rerun the day before New Year's and it was something. Even better than being there in person. All those fancy houses going up like toilet paper. You can't help feeling sorry for those folks, even if they are rich. At the end of the show, the reporter called the Santa Ana the dark angel of the Santa Sangres. I remembered that because it was kind of catchy and it made the wife wonder if he wasn't Catholic after all, even with a name like Steinfelder or something like that. He said he called it a dark angel because the wind brought all that dust and death."

Carl shook his head. "No, it's not the line that's so bad. It's just that those fires can do anything. They're so big and so fast they're not like fires at all. I don't know what they're like."

"And you think we're due?"

"Yeah," Carl grinned at me, "sure as a Chevy. Like I was saying, any time I get an empty feeling in my wallet, I know I'm due some overtime. That wind's going to check in any day now."

As I left the mess hall, something Cominsky hadn't said arranged itself for me. He had made no provision for a Santa Ana without a fire in its wake. Where the wind came, fire followed.

The bunkhouse was quiet when I came in. A few people reading, some asleep, a game of double solitaire. There had been some limp banter in the last few weeks, but nobody's heart was in it. Ever since the dying started, there seemed to be less and less to say. Or reason to say it. For most of us, Pitkin was the first dead person we had seen; maybe, except for Perez and Calendar, the first we'd even known. We didn't have the seasoning to deal with finality.

I followed the metallic clanking around behind the shower room where I knew I'd find Mundeen lifting weights. Another two weeks and he'd be gone, along with Kruger. They'd been able to stay longer this season because their schedule started later than usual. The line coach had said he'd like to farm out the whole team to a hotshot crew for the summer. Mundeen cruised through daily doubles when he reported every fall.

I thought about Cominsky's complaint. Me, Mundeen, and Kruger.

Jarvis was leaving for Humboldt State a week earlier. I didn't know about Orem, but I thought his junior college started about the same time. And then there was Stinson and Moya. They'd be going into the Army in October. It wasn't going to leave Cable much to work with.

Mike was finishing a repetition of military presses. He was wearing a pair of ratty cutoffs and running shoes. At rest, his bulk was deceptive—smooth, continuous, unassertive. Working against the weight, his muscles flared into steep contours, veins bulging and pumping like a network of snakes. He only weighed 225 when he came in at the start of the season. The last time he mentioned it, he was up to 242, close to the size the pro scouts wanted to see him play at his senior year.

I waited out the set without saying anything. Mike didn't talk while he was lifting; it broke his concentration on breathing. When he'd finished, he popped a can of Gatorade and chugged it.

"How's the back?" Last week, Mike was worried that he'd pulled something in his lower back.

"No problem. Just a kink I had to work out."

"I was just talking to Cominsky, about the Santa Anas. You ever been on one?"

"No, I was always back to school by then. I always wanted to take one of those mothers on. Now. . . ." He shrugged and pinched the can in half, an old drinking habit.

"All of us going back to school or the Army is going to leave Cable pretty short."

"He'll manage. Shit, he's short now. I'm not so sure he doesn't like it that way. If he was a coach, he'd probably want to play with eight men. He wants it the hard way. You ever wonder why most crews got a sawyer up front now, running one of those Homelite bow saws? I could rip the brush a new one with one of those honeys, but Cable thinks it'd turn us into pussies. I asked him about it, and he said maybe I'd like a golf cart to get around on the line in too."

"I guess it's pretty slow up north this year. If it really got going, they could pull down some crews from Region 6. Maybe they'd bring in some smokejumpers; they ought to be able to handle themselves."

Mike began to twist his torso in a slow, circular stretching exercise. "Not off what I've seen. I ever tell you about my first season, when they flew us back to Colorado?"

I shook my head.

"We worked three different fires before we got home, but this happened on the first one, the Caliber Creek. It was after our third or fourth shift, and we got into fire camp late. We cleaned up and were waiting in line while they fired up some steaks for us. Then this crew of jumpers comes in off the line. They'd been out fucking around falling snags all day; they thought packing saws made them studs or something. They'd been there as long as we had, but I never did see them cut any line. Anyhow, a couple of them tried to freestyle into the front of the line and we bounced them. Pretty soon, everybody was beating on each other. There wasn't a difference of two or three guys, one way or the other. By the time Cable got over from the timekeepers, we'd flat done a number on them. They shipped them back to Missoula the next morning."

Mike started rotating in the opposite direction. "You got to give them credit for balls, though. I wouldn't jump out of a plane for all the cheerleaders at USC. But once they're on the ground, they're pretty worthless. A bunch of old guys; I mean, some of them must be forty. No staying power. They just want in and out like a rabbit. On a campaign fire you got to keep stroking away for the long haul, not shoot your wad before you even get it out of your pants. I wonder what those guys tell each other about Colorado."

The Colorado story sounded good. From what I knew of Mundeen, it was probably mostly true. Like Mike, I wondered how the story came out at the jumper base in Missoula. It flattered me to be part of a crew whose reputation extended through the West. It was as close to fame as I ever expected to get. Cable told us once that some forest supervisors asked for Dalton when they ordered hotshot crews from Region 5. China Hat and Charley Klister's crew of retread tanker foremen out of Redding got the publicity. Dalton got the job done, season after season, and the overhead knew it.

"It's funny, but I don't feel the same about leaving this year." Mike was stacking his weights up against the building. I wondered how many thousand tons had gone into the making of that body. "Maybe it's because I don't ever figure to be back. Maybe it's just different."

"How?"

Mike didn't answer right away. It wasn't like him to grapple with a response.

"Well, I guess what it comes down to is this season I'm glad to be going."

"You mean, what happened?" For most of us, by now, the deaths and all that surrounded them had resolved into the neutral phrase, "what happened."

"No. I thought about that. That's not it. That's only part of it." Mundeen scuffed at the dirt. "It's like I've just outgrown it. You know, like writing on the wall in the shitter or wondering if other people think you're OK. Something you get over. I guess I'm getting over Dalton."

I hadn't expected anything like this from Mike. It wouldn't be the last time I was reminded that introspection was not the monopoly of people who could toss off the word comfortably in conversation.

"Besides me, I think this place is changing. Jimmy's gone flat creepy on everybody. I don't even think Cable can make any sense out of him anymore. And something's got into Cable too. Whatever it is just keeps hammering away, wearing him down. I can see it looking back, one season to the next. It's not his body, and he hasn't gotten any sweeter. There's just something about, I don't know, shit, the way he feels. It's like the locker room before a game, and everything seems the same, but you know the team is gonna flat lay down and die out there on the field."

"Even if he doesn't think so, he's only human. He had everything it takes, but I've seen all-Americans get off their game one way or another and never pull out of it. They had what it took to get there, but when they slipped they didn't have what it takes to get back. And if he goes, Dalton's just another bunch of jerk-offs. I mean, Cable hasn't had bad material to work with, but it's the coach that makes the team. And I'll tell you, without Cable this team would have trouble playing five hundred ball. I'm gonna be just as glad to get out of here. I don't think I'd come back, even if I'd been figuring on it."

Mike walked off a few steps and turned to piss into the dark. "That make any sense?"

"Yeah," I said. "Is Cable pretty much like the coaches you've had?"

"Yeah, except more so. Those coaches at San Jose, they all came from somewhere and they'll be going somewhere else. They know people. Hired, fired—they can do what they do anywhere. If it doesn't work out, they can sell insurance or something. But him. I can't see Cable suping anywhere else, let alone doing anything else. It's like he's found the one thing he's good at, the one thing he really wants. Running this crew isn't doing him any favors, but I'm pretty sure not running it would kill him."

Mike took an enormous breath and blew it away. "Christ, I must have used up a year's worth of thinking the last couple weeks. For sure I used up a week's worth of words tonight. I haven't talked like this since I silver-tongued Marlene into bed on our third date. Well, maybe when

I had to explain to my old man how half a dozen sheep got locked up in the garage when I was home last Christmas. They were part of a joke I was gonna play on an old high school buddy that never came off. You wouldn't believe what sheep shit smells like, even when you don't feed them anything. Worse than Bailey's pizza."

He was talking himself away from it now, moving out of the zone of uneasiness, the interior. I asked him one more thing.

"What was Jimmy like? Before this season."

"Jimmy? Like a regular Indian."

"That's all?"

"That's all."

Whatever other sad surprises Mike's mind held for him, he was not going to locate them tonight. We dwindled off into talk of football. Mike promised me tickets to his first home game if he made the pros with a West Coast team. I promised to come see him play.

Kruger was coming back from a shower when Mike and I walked into the barracks.

"Hey, Mike, you know what day this is?" Kruger swerved within range of Stonecrofter's bunk and snapped a towel at his bare feet. Nelson jerked them back, but without squeaking— a small victory in a summer full of losing.

"We got out of double digits. Only nine more days till Christmas."

Kruger was the only one of us who showed no effects from what had happened. After denouncing Calendar and Perez, he seemed to dismiss the matter as having nothing to do with him. I don't remember him saying anything about Pitkin. I couldn't see that the summer had altered him in any respect. Which meant that his low grade assholery went on unalloyed.

"Short-timers, you and me." He punched Mike on the shoulder. "Nine more days and we'll be out of this hole, slick as a spic's dick. If I get any shorter, I'll feel like a Mexican-American."

Moya looked at Kruger without expression.

"How about it, Mike, single fucking digit midgets."

"Yeah," said Mundeen. "I'm ready."

Nine days and I'd be gone too.

We must have done some project work that week, but I can't remember what it was. Toward the end, during the Santa Ana alert, we were held at the station. The days were filled with Speyer, with Speyer's talking, layer after layer, his voice curving in and out, spreading into

146

every crevice. It's hard to believe it went on less than a week.

The color in his face became higher, until I imagined he gave off a kind of heat. Yet he never sweated, not even on the line that I saw. The flush that seeped into his face had gone to the side that hadn't been burned. The pallor of the reconstructed side gave his face a harlequin touch, the effect of a mask.

"Who believes in consequence anymore? A few preachers, up in the pulpit, chugging away like old tugboats of the spirit. Hauling empty barges. If one has no guilt, sin is an unfinished equation. Only evil, whatever that is, can believe in goodness, take it seriously. The rest of us are too tepid, too enlightened. Midmost. It only bores us."

"When a person enters his own life wholly, he's meshed in a great mystery. Sealed up in his mind like a monk. Dead ends flanked by sheer dropoffs. By the sound of it, a few mad brother monks, howling prayers down the empty corridors of God. Certainly, everything outside us must be absolutely incomprehensible."

"God must have a mind like an anthill. Think of animals, hit on the road. God plays a game—'What have I got in my hand?' says God. And opens his palm. A deer, a rabbit, an owl. One time, the dull-witted and slow, browsing the odd smell of an oil slick. The next, the pride of the herd: enlarging his foraging range, his harem; just taking a chance on new country. The one, the other. The ants march in and out."

Like this, much of what Speyer said now was disjointed or out of my range or both. But it stuck. Over the years, it would polish so smooth with repetition that the phrases came to resemble some artifact dug up after centuries of use and abandonment— worn with handling beyond recognition.

"Jimmy should be in a gerontology exhibit. At his age, what he can do with his body is hardly less than a miracle of the flesh. But as a medicine man, he's a feeble dose. Oh, Jimmy's a technicolor character and he's got the themes right more or less. But it's as though some anthropologist got hold of him and fed him peyote buttons and hauled him off to see a new-wave Latin American sorcerer film. And turned whatever was genuine about him as an Indian into cigar store metaphysics, ethnic quackery. Who could believe how he talks—'Its doom runners come already before it.' He'd be laughed off the reservation if he said anything like that around Indians. No, he's not remotely authentic. Given this culture, I'm not sure what form an authentic shaman would take. But I think I'd recognize the texture. I've known two, maybe three. I judge him from some experience in the matter."

"A diversion, out here in Gaza, but not necessarily harmless. Who enters into the gods of nature is beyond restraint. Someone that sincere and extravagant. . . . He's erratic enough the calculus of human probability doesn't apply. Everyone is dangerous. Yes, even you, my sentinel friend. But a man whose deviations plot out on no human curve has somehow fooled the odds, has become utterly corrupt. There is no way of predicting what he is capable of."

Scenes from those days surface and sink. Speyer pulling out a handkerchief—the rest of us carried oversized bandanas—dabbing spittle from the corner of his mouth and carefully folding it away. A flock of ravens, dozens of them, rising up from a single rabbit carcass. A metallic smile, as though it had corroded across his face for centuries, whenever I spoke of the future.

"I knew a man once, in Seattle. A fat man. He'd stared down some ugly roads and taken a few of them. I was working at a clinic. It was his third time in. He was a poet. Listen:

Seamless
fire spreads its litany
along the barkskin, finding each crevice:
Mine it chants, *Mine* and *Now*.
Walloping up the slope
ignites its undersong:
More.
Everything.
Logs and rocks tearing free.
Evidence
going up in smoke.

"The man had never seen a wildfire. Imagine it—a mind that can start out with nothing but language and end up at the truth. He used to trade me his poems for things. They take away everything in there, you know. He wrote them in crayon. They wouldn't even let him have a pen."

"What did you trade?"

"Anything he wanted."

Coming in late, small wasps of light beating through a cloudbank far to the west. Our last evening together.

"The world's lie gets into us all, like cancer. Massive doses of honesty won't work against it, not the whole spectrum of regret. To get free, you must cut it out; you must mutilate yourself. Guess how many undertake it. The other side is as wretched. Those synthetic factmongers. Boxcars of information, warehouses of opinion, but never much truth. We ripple in the field between a negative pole and a vacuum. The magnetic gravity of pain, the enormous vacuum of death. Riding what arcs between them—transfixed, crucified, magnificent."

That night, wind fidgeted through the camp, drawing small sounds from the barracks. A light marine chill edged in with it. I had trouble falling asleep. Rustlings moved across the row of bunks as others burrowed deeper into sleep or struggled over the crest of wakefulness.

We woke to odd light. Fog. Coffee took on its winter meaning. The air felt like a different medium, and we moved through it as if in slow motion. Color seemed strained from everything. Speyer's face took on such radiance that whatever fever he had must have crowned then. The contrast with the dead side of his face was striking. Others must have noticed this, although I heard no mention of it.

Cable came into the mess hall while we were still eating. Since Bouquet Canyon, he had been taking his meals alone in his room. The Regional Office had issued a Santa Ana advisory for the Santa Sangre, Los Padres, Cleveland, and San Bernardino National Forests. Cable called off pt. Instead, we rechecked our personal gear and some of us went through the crew equipment on the truck. We kicked the truck's radio on to monitor, and listened as patrolmen and tankers spread out to close all national forest access roads. Old lookouts were opened up and manned, and both patrol planes were up, waiting for the slot, the interval between the fog and wind where they could work. On other channels we could hear the county and state positioning engine companies, rounding up standby crews, filling the airwaves with jittery 10-code, getting ready.

By late morning, the fog had broken into patchy pockets and was sucked back to sea. Where we might not have noticed it before, the air now seemed monumentally calm. All of us, even Kruger, were subdued by the pressure that grew between the urgency out there somewhere and the absence of movement, the silence poised above the ridges, as far into the Santa Sangres as we could see.

I looked for Jimmy after lunch, making a slow circuit of the compound. He wasn't there; I couldn't remember when I noticed him last. Speyer was reading. The afternoon took on weight, and clarity. I was snagged by detail: filaments of bark on a eucalyptus, stipples of rust on the metal roof of the tool shed, the itching clack of a grasshopper, going about its work.

Into the afternoon, we began to manipulate the pressure which was tinted now with boredom. A basketball game, three-on-three; passing around Moya's cache of skin magazines, sleeping. Snead was polishing his Chevy. The Bel Air had the kind of custom paint job that seemed to draw light down through layer after layer of gloss before releasing it in reflection. His tape deck was cranked up all the way, playing The Doors. He had bought bootleg tapes of their concerts, and edited out everything except three performances of "The End." An eerie triptych. Among the decals arrayed on the Chevy's rear bumper was one I hadn't read before. In bold, blue and black graphics, it read: "I WANT TO RISE SO HIGH THAT WHEN I SHIT I WON'T MISS ANYONE." It was paired on the bumper with another addition: "WHEN I DIE BURY ME FACE DOWN SO EVERYBODY CAN KISS MY ASS."

By supper, a different sort of anxiousness had set in. What if this was a mistake? What if the wind wasn't going to come after all? We wanted it now, release from the foreplay of weather. It was a feeling I could trace down, for me, back to grade school. A small town in the plains of South Dakota, watching the December afternoon darken too early, hoping it meant a big storm was coming in and we'd be let out to get home before it broke.

The Santa Ana careened into camp a couple of hours before sunup. All at once. The barracks shuddered with the impact and everyone came awake. Power was out and we dressed in the dark. Cable had told us at supper that if it broke during the night, we should be ready to roll before daybreak. Dressed, gear together, we made our way through the abrasive gusts to the mess hall. Bailey cooked on propane stoves, and we ate by lantern light. Cominsky warmed up the truck and left it idling in front of the mess hall. Cable had said there was a chance, not more than that, that a few minutes could mean the difference between nailing a fire in its tracks and being out of the game entirely.

Just listening to the wind made it plain what an awesome antagonist it would be. And the long thought of it: rising from the desert, finding the high passes, accelerating down the slopes and canyons, pouring out across the coastal plain, topography upping the voltage beyond where measurements mean anything. An elemental imperative. You had to up the ante of language just to think about it in any proportionate terms.

With the lanterns and solemnness, the mess hall took on a sense of sanctuary—the feel of a vessel, old but seaworthy, where we could ride it out. Morning squeezed into the room and we put out the lanterns. It must have been six-thirty or so. In the early light, you could already see the brown and yellow scum that would shield the sky until the wind was done. And even indoors, you could feel the fine grit starting to build in the corners of your eyes. At full light, I saw that Jimmy was in the room, near the wall at the end of one of the trestle tables. On his left cheek were two diagonal stripes, yellow and black.

The call came in around seven. The fire was on the Catlow, not more than a twenty minute run from the station. The compound faded in and out of the dust, the buildings riding like phantoms, as Cominsky got everything out of the gears, slung us through the curves, leaving Dalton. My last view of the station seemed at first a slurring of vision, then slapstick with a chilly undertow. One, then another, then four or five, the tire carcasses had torn free from the obstacle course and crossed the compound, some wobbling wildly, others spinning in perfect balance, careening away from their old context.

The highway was in good shape coming down from camp, although we had to stop once to buck a tree that had fallen across the road. The configuration of the ridges and canyons made it necessary to drop down almost to the valley, parallel the mountains, then loop back up to the fire. There were two east-west routes above Foothill Boulevard. We heard over the radio that one was blocked; we tried the other and found it an impassable tangle of utility poles and snapping wires.

When we got to it, Foothill itself looked hardly possible. Traffic lights were out, and the morning commuters, though fewer than usual, were barely moving. Cominsky hit the lights and siren and we swung out into the eastbound lanes where traffic was spottier. Cars stopped or veered. At one intersection, a highway patrolman waved us through; at another, a city policeman tried to flag us down. We must have navigated seven or eight miles like this, taking whatever the street would give us and when that wasn't enough going up over the curb, taking out some bus benches, tightroping it down the sidewalk.

The ride distracted us from our destination. Snead and Moya evaluated Cominsky's talent behind the wheel. Stinson thought he saw his sister and some friends walking into a store. At every near miss, Kruger let out a long, braying whoop. Across from me, I could see Speyer's face faded from fever back to near white. Next to him was

Mundeen, then Jimmy, just behind the cab, hands pressed flat on his thighs the way they had been that night in the truck when he first talked to me. No one said anything about the stripes on his cheek. In the last weeks, he had gone into an orbit which the crew made no attempt to track.

Finally, we were off Foothill and onto open county road, flat out through a residential area and then between the lips of a canyon, heading back into the Santa Sangres.

The canyon funnelled the wind with such force that we had to hunch down in the back, below the level of the cab, out of the stream. Later, in fire camp, I noticed that the paint on the truck was gone down to bare metal around the grill and the windshield was pitted.

Bent over, I tried to scan the ridges ahead, searching for the span of the fire's column, until I realized that in this wind there would be no column.

A few people were there ahead of us: Oscar, one or two others I recognized from the ranger station, the county engine company stationed at the mouth of the canyon. The fire, started from a downed power line, had been picked up almost immediately by a patrolling power company crew. It had taken us nearly an hour to get there. Already, the fire was over a hundred acres and spreading geometrically, spotting ahead of itself, small blazes breaking out like pox ahead of the main fire. The county pumper was not doing anything. Its intricacies of gauges, plumbing, and hardware, maybe half a million dollars worth of gear, as irrelevant as anything else we'd try that day. Cominsky hadn't shut our truck off, and I noticed that all the other rigs were running.

The fire was named "Backbone." It had started near the boundary of an area set aside by the Forest Service for its geological interest. A major lateral ridge of the Santa Sangres, the Devil's Backbone dominated the area. The ridge was studded with columns of basalt, great slab-sided monuments leaning above slopes of rubble. I remembered seeing slides of the area during our Forest orientation in fire school. In the frame of geologic time, I wondered if these towers would witness anything of consequence as the wind and the fire and the rest of us went about our business here.

Although the ground it covered was plain enough, its rate of spread beyond anything I had seen or imagined, the fire had an ambiguity to it. Blowtorched by the wind, it burned quick and clean. The flow of smoke was inconsequential. I was still in the mistaken habit of partly gauging the caliber of a fire by the amount and density of its smoke. We took a few smarting skiffs as we waited, hardly enough to raise a protective film of tears. Moving with liquid ease, the flames scudded low to the ground, bowed by the wind, diminutive. The whole horizontal format shrunk the fire's sensory impact. It just didn't look, didn't feel, like something beyond contending with.

We didn't get out of the truck. Indirect line would never have held; direct line was impossible. We conceded the canyon to the fire, the first of a sequence of withdrawals as we dropped down out of the canyon and looped west, probing the ridges and ravines, moving first at Oscar's order and later under command of a special Santa Ana Interagency Team, looking for somewhere to check the lateral spread as Backbone outburned what passed for fire forecasting in such conditions. The head of the fire belonged to itself. Before the fire front, only the end of anything combustible made any difference at all.

We saw some action, being shuttled to spot fires catching in patches of brush left as open space in a subdivision of several hundred homes. Husbands, teenagers, some wives even, stood in backyards or on roofs, dribbling water from garden hoses across the expanse of cedar-shingled roofs. The kids jumped around a lot after sparks; their parents looked resolute, terrorized. The water fell limply out of the hoses, pressure gone to less than an urgent piss.

We cut line across vacant lots and in a small, gone-to-seed park, more out of the need to do something than out of much purpose. We won more than we lost on the ground, but the contest was in the air. Rust-colored flecks rode above us, deadly embers embedded with seeds of fire strewn across the cedar tinder roofs. Engine companies patrolled the streets, doing what they could. Backbone would never get closer than half a mile, but its fallout fired a separate and selective holocaust, hemorrhaging across the tract: that one and that one and this. Houses went off through the afternoon, maybe thirty by the time we were shifted west again.

The scenes click like slides projected on a screen that disintegrates under each image. People gathered around a portable TV on the hood of a car, watching one of their neighbors being interviewed. Heaps of belongings on the lawns and driveways, crammed into cars, set adrift on air mattresses in swimming pools frosted with clots of ash. A woman languidly leading a zebra down the street by a halter; a man with a pistol screaming at an engine company captain. A transcontinental moving van pulling away from a house, the trailer bouncing, no weight to it. An old man in his yard, just standing still.

West again, back into the brush, we finally got our teeth into some real line. After a day of stuttering, the clarity and long rhythm of cutting felt good. We worked on into the night and through it, punching a line up the bed of a dry arroyo, so far from the fire we couldn't even smell it. Only its leprous glow in the eastern sky kept us company, never more than a twist of your head away.

No one relieved us when we were pulled off the line in the morning. The line tied into nothing—it simply ended where we left off. Through the haze of fatigue, a sullen thought surfaced: someone had made a mistake or strategy had altered out from under us. The line, a throwaway.

Fire camp had been set up on the football field of a local high school. The grass was pleasant, and the chance to shower, even in cold water. But the field lay open to the wind, and it drove across unbuffered. We took the cots we were issued, turned them on their sides, and staked them down for windbreaks. What sleep we got came tucked behind the popping canvas.

Cable mustered us up for supper late in the afternoon. The food tasted as though the cooks had mutinied after trying to just keep the stoves lit, much less cook on them, and the meal had been finished by whatever stray hands could be rounded up. Everything was impartially garnished with the wind's grit. We tanked up on milk and fresh fruit.

Oscar came to see us before we headed out. He moved and spoke like a man in pain—his district, his crew, his fire. Technically, he was not in charge. In every other way, it was his. In Washington, the statistics on Backbone would be microscopic entries on a computer disk. For Oscar, the losses would be inscribed on the raw tissue of memory.

He told us how things stood: six thousand acres, give or take, no estimate of containment; the Santa Ana continuing at least through tomorrow; the Region spread thin trying to cover other fires. He told us tonight could make a difference of ten thousand acres—habitat, watershed, living country. He said he had argued us into a sector where it mattered most, where he would hesitate sending any other crew. And he said it was going to be bad.

As we loaded into the truck, I stood apart for a moment, rewrapping my headlamp cord. A quirk of the wind brought their voices to me.

"Besides that, Bob, you're short men. I don't have to tell you not to take chances."

"Then don't."

"You know what I mean."

"Every time out is a chance."

"Good luck."

"See you in the morning."

Driving out to our jump-off point, the sun going down swollen in the malarial sky, we passed an improbable menagerie, a herd of tankers strung out along a mile or so of county road. Lights flicking and strobing, engines breathing in and out, they were arrayed for a tanker stand or to support a major backfiring. Gray and olive, green, blue, white, orange, yellow, the whole spectrum of red; a gathering of beasts, come in common cause to confront the predator. Forest Service and State Division of Forestry tankers, four-wheel drive county brush tankers and regular engine companies, pumpers from maybe a dozen cities, National Guard, Navy, and Air Force fire rigs, Civil Defense units, construction water trucks, Department of Sanitation septic pumpers, Highway Division nurse tankers, flatbed trucks with slip-on tanks from the state's mosquito control program, a water truck from the Calaveras Circus. Rig after rig, like the boats at Dunkerque, the muffled pulse of water circulating, engines, pumps, and suction; the urgent curve of tension arcing from the men in the cabs, up the ridges and beyond, out through the brushfield to where the fire was coming down.

West, the county road dead-ended. We left it for a brushy fire spur that vanished altogether for stretches. We lost it navigating the rock rubble delta of an arroyo, picked it up on the other side, and finally parked the truck where the spur merged with a fresh cat line, coming in from the west and veering here, up a ridge and out of sight. Cupped away from the wind, we still squinted out of reflex. Higher up, we took it full force again, dust streaming away from our feet as we waded up through the soil torn loose by the cat. Our night's work would begin as far up the ridge as the skinner could push his machine.

The sector lay along the crest of one of the rib ridges of the Devil's Backbone, striking down, perpendicular, toward the valley. The ridge fell away sharply on both sides and was rooted with a heavy growth of chamise and manzanita, broken here and there by rock croppings and thinning where the brush shaded into the bulk of the Backbone.

We met the cat churning back the way it had come. The skinner looked bored. Standing beside him, bucking and yawing, a Forest Service man clutched the cage, looking seasick. The cat throttled back and Cable swung up on the treads.

As the dusk took hold we could see, across two miles to the east, the line of the next ridge standing out against the level glow of the fire working its back slope. To the north, odd, evening cumulus had begun to lumber up somewhere beyond the Backbone, out over the desert face of the Santa Sangres. Away from the drift of the diesel fumes, the oil from the brush gave off an acid, urine smell, as though some great beast had marked its territory here. Cable cast off from the cat and it tracked away down the ridge.

Cable laid it out for us. We were looking at a mile and a half of cutting, extending the line up the ridge and tying it in to a mammoth rockslide on the western flank of the Backbone. At the first drop in the wind, they would backfire, trying to funnel everything down to where the tankers waited.

We rigged up our headlamps while Bob rehearsed escape routes: back down the line, over the side into the next canyon, and a last choice—breaking through the fire front and finding a burned-out spot where you would get scorched but not, perhaps, burned up. Always meticulous, Cable seemed more thorough than usual. I registered the escape routes on automatic pilot. I was thinking about ending up like last night, no fire in sight, sweat chilling to shivers whenever we stopped moving. Unless something happened, it didn't look like we were going to see any hot line tonight. Despite what Oscar had said, counting on that was probably the only reason we were out here. On some fire behavior specialist's model, this chunk of line must have been drawn in ice blue ink.

We swung into the work, centered on the ridge's axis, balanced between the light feathering out of the sky in the west, the rising illumination of fire to the east. Working out the stiffness, we settled into our rhythm, a purposeful trance of motion that held fatigue in suspension. Bob set the pace at lead hook. Tonight he went out fast, sealed in the rhythm, pushing hard. Behind him, Jimmy hooked in counterpoint, hermetic, submerged somewhere beneath our common trance. Speyer seemed less easy than before. I had an odd sense of him ranging outside the cadence: intense, alert, aware beyond the precise wedging arc of his hook. I threw the brush they cut, and as night settled, the world was bound within our narrow track through the brushfield, the pale circle of light from my headlamp. Beyond that rim, the even dark closed around the brush I hurled into it.

We took our first break around midnight. When the tools had been sharpened, we sat with our headlamps out: smoking, drinking a little water, not saying much, watching. The fire had come over the ridge to the east and was working its flank, tacking down laterally across the wind, filaments of flame raveling the slope. Nearly opposite us, it reached a bench and made a fingering run. Small eddies of paler fire plumed up, spun above the bank of flames, and disappeared. Fire spores carried downwind, infecting the brushfield. A prodigious dance of fire, extravagantly choreographed by temperature, humidity, fuel, slope, and wind. And above the blowing of the Santa Ana, across nearly a mile, we listened to the steady mammoth roar of its coming.

Although the fire was below us, the wind was our margin of safety, bearing the main firefront away downcanyon. The fire still seeped diagonally down the slope, but it absorbed distance so slowly I could hardly measure its progress. Before the break, I had noticed the brush thinning out a little. Ahead, I could make out the Backbone, opaque against the fainter dark of the sky. I guessed one, maybe two hours, and we'd tie in at the top. Maybe the wind would drop before our shift was over. I wanted to backfire from our line, setting the scorpion against itself. Turning away, we embedded ourselves in the trance of the work that remained.

Then something was wrong, the trance lifting. Its sturdy balance of force, resistance, release had shifted and the rhythm came apart for me, undone by a loose fear that I had forgotten something important, left it behind, and now would be lost.

The wind had quit. Down the line, cutting slowed, then stopped as each of us surfaced into the perfect calm. Left alone by the wind, the fire frittered, but came perceptibly now down the slope, its perimeter extending in thrusts and bulges. The slope was veined with small draws, and as the flames intersected these they sluiced up them, turning the chutes into flumes of fire.

In the growing light, Cable looked reflective, as though he were trying to remember something. He must have been lining up odds: Dalton—the legend and us—against what remained to be done, against the pathology of all those fires, against this one. We could go out easily now down the line. Or we could go on. If the Santa Ana came up, the fire would heel over again and there would be plenty of time. Without the wind, we still might tie the line in before the fire reached the canyon bottom, perhaps in time to go out our line backfiring. With luck, we could turn the fire here, maybe finish it. If the fire crossed the canyon, all bets were off. We would have minutes, then, to bail off the back side of the ridge, wading down through the brush before the fire crested the ridgeline. Even the cat line wouldn't hold against a run on this slope.

Cable called for our two-minute drill. Mundeen had given it the name—a fourth quarter drive against the clock. We would slit a scratch line to the top, the chancy minimum; then back down the line, unraveling fire behind us as we came.

We turned again to the brush, urgency and control beveling to the edge we had to have. The ridge was flushed with light, and we began to pick up radiant heat from across the canyon. The fire pulse plunged through the arteries of brush and we could feel its swell beat against us. Quirky winds veered across the steady suck of oxygen into the flames, the fire making its own weather now. I worked with absolute focus, as though one wrong act might make the difference. But gradually, at first against my will, some part of me drew away, enlarging until at last it seemed to take in the whole hulk of the Santa Sangres, the vast, impassive brushfields, the furnace stoking itself; beneath and beyond, the night going on and on. And fourteen mortal men, flickers of flesh: negligible, there, remarkable beyond all accounting.

Then the firefront was into the canyon bottom. Too soon. And the Santa Ana was back, not full force, but with strength to deflect the head perhaps enough. And Cable hesitated, squinting into the canyon. No way of backfiring now, only the chance that without the momentum of a straight run up the ridge, the fire might not breach the line. If the line was all there. And we were so close now, so deep into this line, this season. More variables, the wrong certainties piling up, the whole configuration tilting, but the equation still possible. And Cable turned his back on the pouring light. And we went on.

And from this turning I remember a whole, simultaneous; sequence only because the mind insists on continuity, divided from time by the heat which came first in surges and then with the steady, molten force of an open forge. Smoke boiled across the line, eddied, and came again leaving us staggered and stung. Jimmy into a high, keen singing. No compression, no finesse, cutting from passion fused with panic. Desperate with exhaustion, choking for air in a fragment of clearing—a sound, a dry staccato clicking and a jag of terror through me above my level fear of the flames. Cable, Jimmy, Speyer, me: in a charmed circle of clear air we pivoted toward the buzzing. A diamondback, driven by the fire, lay coiled near Jimmy, tongue flickering, neck tensed back. Jimmy, leaning, cocking his hook, belt hanging free, buckle gone. Swinging as the snake struck, splitting gristle and bone. Rigid as the fangs went in above his boot. And held. Slowly, turning, his hook into a great circle above his head hurled at Speyer; then off the ridge, lunging down, screeching, into the fire. Speyer on one knee, missed. A crouch beyond reflex. The slope of fire, waves of flame surging and cresting its surface. Then a luminous globe, spinning out from the firefront, pale blue streamers behind, wheel of fire. Cable speaking into the radio, a deep stain down the elbow of his shirt, saying we were taking casualties, saying we needed the helitack medical team when they could get off the ground, saying we were seven chains short and it didn't look like we'd be able to tie the line in. I stood, dead center, pierced by the end of Jimmy's wail, a silence into which no words could ever be spoken. Cable's hands on me, steady, but moving me back and forth—the hook, the hook clattered into some rock behind the line, find it, never leave a weapon, we might still, it might get us out. And away from me into the smoke where others had clustered. Mechanically, stiff-legged to keep them from buckling, through the brush: a bare patch of scaly shale, the rigid sparwork of dead brush, the hook. Turning back; not going back, I think, only turning. There. Down the line, rising out of the firestorm, a fire whirl: malignant, swollen beyond itself, beyond natural law, into a fire spout funneling up hundreds of feet. Tilting, coming up the ridge, a pulse of white flame at its center, riding the edge of the fire; lateral sheets of flame drawn to its base, shreds of burning brush hurled far across the line. Spot fires coming up around me, the back side of the ridge breaking out. Speyer. In a thinning of smoke, at the end of our line, as far as we had come. Fading and coming back in the smoke-clotted light—a darkening, a density, the mouth of a tunnel in the mountain of smoke. And the fire spout, spasming free, a convulsion of flame bending to him. Who did not run but waited, faced into it, not burning yet but as a man lit by his bones, luminous. Bulky smoke took me down, blinded. On the ground I could breathe a little. Scuffing around on my knees, keeping my back to it as the worst heat came from one way and another, I sloshed my canteens over my shirt and jeans, the last of it on my bandana. Someone screaming "no no no no no no no." A voice so gone in terror and pain it seemed unshaped by a human mouth. Yanked my shirt up where my neck was blistering. The orange rolled out, down my thigh. A little clown. Heat steamed my lungs as I gagged for air. Tearing at the orangehide till it came apart. A chunk stuffed in my mouth, my nose jammed in the rest. Whining against the pain in my hands. The bandana, knotted, finally, across my face. In a huddle against the earth, rigid, jerking. The fire roar closed.

In the ashen light before full dawn, I slanted in and out of the shallows of consciousness. My body jolted with pain; my mind, treasonous, saying "let go, let go." Lucid, I thought to crawl to the line, to the others, to be found when the rescue team came up. To move an arm blinded me with fibers of light; moving more, I passed out. I tried for the hook, to prop it up, to tie my scorched bandana to it as a sign. My mind eddied away in pain; coming back, I could not remember what I had been trying to do. I lay still then, listening to the rasp of my breath. As I seeped towards death, in focus beyond my filmy sight was the panorama of earth and sky I had inhabited earlier in the night. My last act on the ridge was to resist that sanctuary; my last awareness, if I left my body for it, this time I would not be back.

———

X

When Cable radioed in, the fire boss had rolled two Forest Service medical teams and alerted the burn ward at Los Angeles County Hospital. It was three in the morning, and the Santa Ana, though starting to break down, still gusted to seventy. None of the helicopters in fire camp was equipped to fly at night, much less in that kind of wind. But when Cable's radio went dead, the fire boss woke up a contract pilot who'd pulled a tour flying Cobra gunships in Vietnam. He didn't have to ask him. The pilot got his ship up, but the wind drove him sideways across the heliport, tilting the Sikorsky until the main rotor caught the ground. There was no fire, and the pilot and volunteers—three emergency medical technicians from the overhead team and a helitack foreman—were roughed up but unharmed. The pilot was ready to try another ship. The fire boss called it off.

The ground teams had gotten as far as the line of tankers where the fire held them. Oscar and an L. A. County burn team tied in with them while they waited. Blowtorched, brush burns quickly. Before dawn, the teams had driven through to where we had left our truck and were headed up.

They found most of the crew on the line. Cavenaugh died before anything could be done. Moya—blind and euphoric, nerve ends burned away—lasted long enough for the morphine to ease his way out. They found Stinson alive under Cable's body. Gridding the area, they found more bodies, then me. Weaving through my delirium, I remember the face of a black man on the team, remember wondering if my eyes had been scorched. And trying to explain why I wasn't on the line, that I hadn't been running away. And a refrain, softly, from someone I couldn't see, as they worked on me: "Oh shit, oh shit, oh shit."

The National Guard horsed a big Chinook in on the ridge. Stinson died in the air. The hospital, prepared for fourteen men, got one.

It took hours to locate Jimmy. Speyer's body was never found.

The lead men of a regional investigation team got there in the afternoon. They took photographs and marked the location of bodies. The wind was still too high to risk another helicopter. Dalton went back down the ridge by hand, one by one, the rubber body bags making small squishing sounds as they swayed and faintly ticking as the wind buckshot them with grit.

My burns were serious, but once they got an IV started on the ridge and brought me out of shock, they didn't think they'd lose me. I had second-degree burns over my butt and the backs of my thighs and calves; third-degree on one wrist along a gap between my leather glove and the cuff of my fire shirt, on one ear and the side of my neck, and in a semicircle around my waist where the elastic of my shorts had melted and stuck to the skin. My lungs had been singed, and they pumped me with antibiotics that checked the pneumonia. There was an early skin graft on my neck, a touch-up graft later, and some reconstructive work on my ear. Everything healed. Even the pain was routine. I was off the critical list in four days, out of the hospital in three weeks.

The doctor who flew in on the Chinook—and, later, the Forest Service investigation team—pieced it together for me. Apparently, the area where Jimmy's hook landed had been burned over in a spot lightning fire earlier in the season. It gave me a margin of forty feet or so where there was nothing for the fire but me. The fire shirt and hard hat, my wet jeans and bandana, and staying down gave me maximum protection. But it was the orange, the doctor said, that probably saved my life. Breathing through its pulp must have filtered the worst of the heat. Without it, he said, my lungs would have been seared; I would have suffocated. He wanted to know how I came to use the orange that way. I had no answer.

My mother and father flew in for a week. Oscar saw me twice, but it was hard on both of us. Pending a formal Forest Service investigation, we couldn't talk about what happened. There wasn't much else to say.

Raylene saw me a few days before I was released. Coming in, she had a light sheen of moisture on her neck and shoulders and her musky perfume overrode the antiseptic air. She asked me what happened and I told her.

"It had to be like that; I don't think he could have lived with it, losing everything. Bobby used to say they paid him to do two things—put out fires and keep the crew in one piece. Losing Pitkin was real hard on him. I know he treated you like men, and he expected you to work like men. But he thought about you like kids, like somebody's kid brother. Cable could always look out for himself. I don't think he tried to get out."

I couldn't think of anything to say. Raylene started talking again. After Korea, she said, Cable couldn't get it up anymore. Mostly, she said, it was all right, but sometimes she needed something more and that was all right too. I couldn't read her eyes behind her sunglasses.

"One arm and a dishrag cock, he was more man than most women ever get. I was lucky, I guess. We both got what we wanted. I can't change what I want; I guess what you do is change what you settle for."

I told her I was going to Oregon for a few weeks when I got out of the hospital—find a mattress of moss by a stream and let the Cascades seep into me. I asked her to come.

"You're a sweet kid, and God knows I'm sucked close to dry. But me and all this, we feed on each other. I'd die in a decent place. Besides," she squeezed me affectionately on the thigh and I yipped in pain, "you're not going to be rolling around on any mattresses for a while."

Just before she left, I said something about Speyer.

"You know, Cable thought a lot of the guy for a while. It's funny, because it turns out he was queer. Bobby said he even made a pass at him once."

"What did Bob do?"

"He didn't say, but he must not have messed him up too bad or you guys would have seen it."

Raylene gave me a solid kiss on the lips. "You come by the Midway anytime and we'll beat some balls around the table. I'll buy you a good drunk. What happened, happened. You forget about it and get on with your life. I can remember for both of us. I'm cut out for that. Well, keep it handy and keep it happy."

She wrinkled her nose at me and smiled and was gone.

The Forest Service investigation team interviewed me my last day in the hospital. The fire staff officer from Region 6 was in charge. With him were the assistant forest supervisor of the Santa Sangre, a fire behavior specialist from the Region 5 fire laboratory, a hotshot superintendent from Region 3, and an imperially cordial, largely silent deputy chief from the Washington Office that everyone deferred to. The assistant forest supervisor, a balding man with an audibly inclement stomach, ran two tape recorders during the interview. The Region 6 man asked most of the questions, reading them from some script he brought with him. He began by leading me through some background information, but mostly they wanted to know about the sequence of Cable's decisions, how they related to the fire's own sequence. The fire lab man tried to clarify my account of the fire's behavior, but my memory of that was not precise enough to be very helpful. After a while, I decided he was mainly trying to impress the deputy chief.

Most of the questions were neutral, almost hypothetical, as though it could have been any Forest Service superintendent under discussion. As the session went on, they became more pointed. Did I notice anything out of the ordinary in his behavior? Did he seem slow, confused, slurred, erratic? Did Cable ever lose control of the crew, of himself? I began to get the drift: they were looking to settle the blame. If it could be made Cable's fault, if they could claim he went haywire, then the organization was protected. Everybody's career was safe.

"He was a damn good sup. He did everything he could. Nobody could have done anything more."

The assistant forest supervisor looked alarmed.

"You don't have the experience to make that judgment," the Region 6 man said coldly. "That's for us to decide."

The deputy chief made a broad, conciliatory gesture. "We're responsible for covering all the bases, you understand. We're trying to learn anything we can to help us avoid this kind of tragedy in the future. I'm sure Bob would have wanted that. And I want to thank you for your cooperation. You've been very helpful; I know this wasn't easy for you."

He signalled the assistant forest supervisor who shut off the tape recorders. "We can tie up any loose ends in the field tomorrow."

The next morning I flew in with them to the ridge. The sky was a stunning blue, the air so vivid it was as though we flew through a dome of crystal. Coming in, I could see Dalton's line branding the ridge, the small distance between the line's end and the rockslide. From our line, ridge after ridge, the land was a sullen gray. The downwash of the helicopter billowed ash and grit as the pilot set us down. Gaudy plastic ribbons streamed from tall metal stakes until the engine was shut down. They marked the locations of bodies. I thought back to our ribboned obstacle course. Nothing here for the ants.

We were accompanied by some technician who followed me around with a tape recorder and directional mike. I was able to answer more of the fire behavior specialist's questions. I tried to gauge where I had last seen Speyer. The fire behavior man said they would make one more sweep of the area, but that a fire spout could generate temperatures beyond 3,000 degrees. Even bones, he said, are combustible in that kind of heat.

Before we flew out, I walked away from them, back to the place where I hadn't died. I waited for the right gesture to occur. Nothing happened. A blue ribbon hung from the metal post. It meant that the man found here had lived.

The Region 3 hotshot superintendent came over after a bit. His name was Slocum. Years later, in Wyoming, I was his division boss on a fire.

"I just wanted you to know what the score was. I think you got a right." He stubbed his boot against the post, and worked a wad of tobacco around in his cheek. "They hauled me out here to make it all look square, like Cable was getting a fair shake. If they decide to pin this on Cable, I can't do nothing about it and neither can you. Washington is still chewing on that shot he lost on Bouquet Canyon. Also, they turned up a bunch of prescriptions for painkillers in his office. It sounds like they can work it out that the pills screwed him up enough to make a difference. That way Uncle's off the hook for jacking you in there in the first place. You were here. I been an inch away more than once. I heard what you said, and now I've seen the ground. I'm not saying I wouldn't have done it different. And I'm not saying he couldn't have pulled it off. You can never tell. But once that fire spout cooked up, you were finished. When your luck turns like that, there's not one damn thing you can do. You and me, we know. But that don't make no difference to them unless they make up their minds they want it to."

Slocum leaned and spit a glob of juice.

"There's one thing bothers me though, and I'd be lying if I didn't say so. I heard a tape of his last transmission. He sounded OK. He sounded like he was calling in for the time of day. But he was asking for artillery. He was calling for a strike on top of his position."

The helicopter's turbochargers began their climbing whine and we turned back toward the ship.

"I guess you know they'd hang my ass out to dry if they found out I told you this."

"Thanks," I said.

In the end, the team's report didn't single out Cable. There was no mention of the painkillers, nor his last radio message. They did hold him accountable for not backing off as soon as the Santa Ana started breaking down and in that, I guess, they were right.

Still, so much of it was beyond his control, beyond his knowing even. The Santa Ana had started to break up treacherously two days before the meteorologists had predicted. The line scout had missed the stand of frost-killed California Oak in the canyon bottom. The fire got into their crowns and bridged across to our ridge far faster than would have happened in pure brush. And the fire spout: that burning at the margin of the natural world, like a judgment out of the Old Testament. It closed the circle on Dalton, cutting off the back side of the ridge as our way out.

The investigation team got these contingencies into the report. They managed to suggest that much of what happened was a result of what might once have been called acts of God. They conveyed this, of course, in passive voice and nonattributive syntax, with jargoned vocabulary like a radioactive mutant of ordinary language. God himself was never actually mentioned.

The report also pointed out that the crew was undermanned, that there was some question whether we should have been sent up the ridge under any circumstance, and, as nearly as I could make out from the prose, that there had been general breakdowns in communication. So in the end there was no blame, or blame spread so thinly it rippled the placid surface of the Forest Service only for those attuned to bureaucratic nuance.

Oscar blamed himself, though the report mentions him only in passing. Had he lived, Cable would have insisted, I think, on taking full responsibility. Which is very different than being set up to absorb blame. As long as they had worked for the government, muffled in the swaddle of collective decisions, jacketed with the minute chain mail of regulation, neither Bob nor Oscar had lost his sense that a man ought to count for something—that counting meant believing actions had consequences, and that consequences had a content that added to or took away from the moral weight of a man. The Forest Service, it turns out, has a surprising number of such men, though few seem to sustain this quality once they leave the field to follow their careers downtown. It is more than a pastel romance of environmentalists that affiliation with the land teaches accountability.

The Bell lifted off the ridge, pivoted south, and headed back to Arcadia, nose tilted down like a hound. The man from the fire lab was telling me about some fire shelters that were under development. Made of high-strength foil, they could be shaken out into a protective envelope if a man was going to be overrun by fire. Another couple of years, he said, and this never would have happened.

The assistant forest supervisor was explaining to the deputy chief how the Santa Sangre was going to rehabilitate the burn. The deputy chief said he wanted the matter given the highest priority. The congressman from this district happened to sit on the House Agriculture Committee. The congressman had heard from a lot of angry voters whose homes had burned up. The congressman wanted to know what the Forest Service was doing with its appropriations. When the rains came this winter, the deputy chief said, he didn't want to hear about more houses lost in floods and mudslides. The deputy chief said he wished he could give away some Region 5 national forests to the Bureau of Land Management. The BLM loved brushpatches, and nobody much cared what they did with them. He slapped the Santa Sangre man on the thigh so he would know it was a joke. He also said Washington was going to be changing the fire culture by changing the nomenclature. Next season, fire bosses would be called incident commanders which should rein in cowboys like Cable.

Below, the Backbone Burn marked the Santa Sangres like the smudged print of an ancient beast—fossil evidence that something awesome had passed this way. The deputy chief unwrapped a piece of gum and flicked the foil wrapper out into the slipstream.

I went back to the hospital that afternoon for a final checkup before they released me. My doctor said he wanted me to come back in if certain symptoms turned up. When I told him I'd be in Oregon for a while, he gave me the name of a friend from medical school who was in practice in Portland.

"You were lucky out there," he said, "and you were luckier in here. You landed the number three burn man on the West Coast, just ask my accountant. Next time you're invited to a barbecue though, you'd better find out what's on the menu first."

America's hospitals, I thought, must be filling up with young doctors who scheduled their patients around M*A*S*H rather than their golf games.

I signed out at the desk and picked up my property. Oscar had brought my gear down from Dalton. He'd taped a note to my fire pack asking me to leave it and any other government gear in the hospital property room. As I pulled some clothes out of the pack, a tuft of gray and white feathers floated free and circled down to the tile. I thought first that a kangaroo rat had started a nest, but I shook out the rest of my clothes and there was nothing else. When I picked up the tuft, I saw that it had been bound together with some kind of sinew or fiber. Whatever it was, I bequeathed it to whoever would inherit my pack next season.

I walked to the parking lot where they had brought my car, and dumped my gear in the trunk. I eased behind the wheel, started the engine, and sat, idling, as something came loose in me. It felt like freedom—all the possibilities north from here. And it felt slack and vacant. The end of some purpose. The end of my season.

So I outlived that fire season, then mostly outgrew it. But it laid down a core that shaped the rings of succeeding years. When the heart is laid down, nothing can ever be the same. The past is foreclosed; the future, configured. Bark, cambium, sapwood—they circle in layers, season by season, that heartwood; my life contoured by Dalton.

I sifted those ashes like an archivist, and by the time I left Humboldt State I had settled enough of it to be able to take Raylene's advice and get on with the rest of my life. Cable might have skidded at the end, but only at the end. Backbone was going to pay Pitkin back to him. And it had been possible; almost to the last we might have done it. We trusted what Cable knew about fire and about us, and we trusted ourselves as a crew. Drawing to fill his straight, Cable bet more than he could cover, risked more than we could afford to lose.

As for Kelly, I think she stumbled into something over her head with the tarot. Not the future, but herself. The cards fell a certain way and she read holocaust into them. She happened to be right; sometimes people are. My roommate my senior year at Humboldt paid his way through college by working the carnival circuit, performing in a magic act with his uncle. Wally could read minds, extract people's pasts, make small objects behave like animated cartoons. He showed me, or told me, how he did it. It was astonishing, but it was ordinary—an ingenious tinkering with our perceptions of this world, crossing no boundaries.

And I came to accept that better men died while I, spun on the wheel by an implausible collusion of act and accident, survived. At Humboldt, I liked the tangible course work in forestry, liked the boots and jeans field work, liked a lot of the people who wanted the woods for a living. I thought I'd see more country, in more ways, in the Forest Service; could, perhaps, stand a little on the side of the land against the coming of numbers.

It has turned out that way, more or less. Even fire held nothing for me I couldn't stare down or sweat out.

Still, there are two ghosts of memory, almost palpable, that have accompanied me. Speyer and Jimmy feel as alive to me now as they ever were. Perhaps it is because they had dimension, an amplitude that seals them beyond the decay of time.

They are with me tonight, as mist sifts over the ridges and rain spreads like a benediction. I have probed again and again, no doubt altering their shape in memory. I have been as careful as I know how, but there is no one to check this against. I am my only source, my own story, my solitary auditor. They are in my hands, as I am in theirs. Linked like binary stars, Speyer and Jimmy circle each other, their center of gravity beyond surmise, their acts in the mortal world tangible as ball lightning, as luck or love. And as inexplicable.

Tonight, at Oscar's desk, rubbing the old itch of my wrist scar, I look out into the rain I cannot see, think of the warm weight of my wife as she curls in bed, listening through sleep for the sound of my truck in the drive. Beneath the rain, the Santa Sangres swarm with the coming of a new season; behind the rain, the world curves away beyond my season of vision.

ACKNOWLEDGMENTS

Excerpts from *Fire Season* have appeared in different form in *Writers Forum, Higher Elevations: Stories from the West* (Swallow Press/Ohio University Press), *Line of Fall* (University of Iowa Press), *Poetry Northwest,* and *Harm* (University of Nevada Press).

www.ingramcontent.com/pod-product-compliance
Lightning Source LLC
Chambersburg PA
CBHW020523120726
47904CB00003B/941